Marcus

A Black Lily Club

Story

BY

CHELLE

Published by Hot Ink Press

Cover by SK Whiteside

Chapter 1

At last I received an invitation to The Black Lily. After two months of waiting to get into this private BDSM club, I'll be there tonight at nine. For two weeks I've done nothing but prepare for this evening, down to every last detail. Even my bikini wax turned more into a full body wax, but the club made their expectations perfectly clear.

I'm taking no chances and following all of their guidelines to the letter. This morning the outfit I'm to wear arrived with a black lily and a note explaining I'm to wear what is in the box and nothing else. Twice they reminded not to forget the lily. Along with my attire, I'm required to fill out consent forms and medical release papers. Everything is official.

With the outfit they gave me leaving nothing to the imagination, I've chosen to wear my hair down in an effort to cover me somewhat. However, the black corset with the blood red laces in the front and back does make me look curvy and sexy all in one nicely tied package. The skirt, if you can call it that, is nothing but a small slip of satin that barely covers my ass. Though I can hardly walk in the 'fuck-me' five inch black patent leather strappy shoes, they accentuate my legs to perfection. I look damn good in this outfit and whoever picked it out has amazing taste.

With no idea who sent the invitation, I grab my coat and the lily and head out the door, having no idea who sent the invitation. I start the car and head down the street and my mind wanders as to what this night will hold.

How does a thirty-year-old woman get to this point?

I'm pretty successful in everything I do, well, everything except relationships. I run my own store making and selling body care products. I run an Internet site for the purchase of my products and teach classes on the uses of herbs and plants for homeopathic remedies.

While I don't claim to be a model, I'm not bad looking by any means, but most men are looking for a damsel in distress, not one who can take care of herself. My last so-called relationship only lasted six months over three years ago. James was a little rough around the edges. Well more than a little. A typical man, he wanted me to sell my business because it took time away from him and his needs. Though he may have wanted a maid and chef, he couldn't afford to pay the bills on his own. He didn't want to take care of me, he just wanted me around for his own selfish needs. I told him that on his way out the door after a fight about my business, and haven't heard from him since. Not that I mind.

I'm not sure what is wrong in my relationships anyway. When it comes to men, something is missing. In the past I've been called frigid or cold, and I just can't seem to let go during sex. I get off alone so there isn't something medically wrong with me, but I can't get there with a guy, no matter what he does. Some tried more than others. Maybe, this bondage club is what I need. At this point, anything is worth a try. If I don't figure something out, I'm going to end up with my battery-operated boyfriend.

The outside of the club is dark and uninviting, more like an empty warehouse, than somewhere to fulfill sexual desire. I don't know much about this place except it is invitation only. Until now I never gave it a second thought how they determine who gets invited.

Now it's a little late for worries, I'm here. The parking lot has minimal lighting, a misty fog rolls across the edges by the forest. I've never seen anything in the news about illegal activities and they have never been investigated. They wouldn't still be open if it wasn't mildly safe, right? I park my car by one of the overhead lights closest to the door and lock the doors.

With a deep breath I steady my nerves, grab my purse and lily off the roof of the car, and head to the entrance.

The tallest man I've ever seen holds the door open for me. He must be at least six foot eight inches tall and built like a brick wall. He's wearing black leather pants that fit like a second skin and his black t-shirt ripples with his every movement.

"Invitation." He holds his hand out.

"Yes." Caught in a stare, his voice jolts me back to reality, and I hand him the invitation.

"Do you have your consent form and medical release papers?"

With a shaking hand, I surrender the paperwork. There is no backing out now.

He ushers me in the door, files the papers and flashes me a predatory smile that does nothing to quell the butterflies dancing in my stomach.

"This way, Miss." He motions for me to follow.

We go through another doorway, into a dimly lit hall. The bass from the music inside vibrates through my bones.

"Take the door at the end of the hall to the barroom. You may have one alcoholic drink at the bar tonight, whatever you wish. The man that sent your invitation will be with you shortly." He nods and shuts the door to the office.

Alone in the hallway, I assess my surroundings. Wrought iron sconces line the corridor dimly lighting the worn stonewalls. I feel like a sacrifice walking to meet the dragon at the edge of the cliff. My breath hitches as my footsteps echo down the long hall.

The closer I get to the door at the end of this tunnel, the louder the music gets. The second I enter the bar I freeze. Nothing here is what I expected for a BDSM bar. Smoke covers the floor, making me feel as if I'm on a cloud. The strobe light makes people look like they're blinking in and out of existence. The huge wooden bar almost covers the length of the wall, and tables are spread along the outer edges of the room with plush booth seats.

In the middle of the room people dressed like me are dancing and mingling together. Thus far this reminds me of an upper class nightclub.

As someone who doesn't frequent bars or nightclubs,

especially on my own, I make my way to the bar, sit, and order a glass of red wine.

Thus far I don't understand why this place is touted as BDSM, it's just like every place else I've been. I lean back on the bar stool, twirling the lily and study the people dancing. Upon closer look, I finally spot a difference, not so much with the club, but the people. Some are wearing collars with leashes attached and some have whips on their hips.

I take a gulp of the wine in an attempt to calm my nerves and stop myself from running back to my car. This is not like me at all. I've never been on a blind date or tried any kind of bondage. While the idea has always appealed to me, I've never had the courage to try. I'm not sure I can completely give up control or let go during sex. I'm always concerned about where to put my hands, questioning if he enjoys what I'm doing, second-guessing every move I make. I lose the moment and never get any pleasure.

Though I can communicate well in my personal life, I can't talk about sex. I don't know how to tell a guy what I like or want. What if it turns him off? What if he doesn't do it right and I still don't get off? Then I just look uninterested at the least, at the most I look like someone who has no idea what they're doing having sex in the first place.

I sit up. This was a bad idea, I should go. I don't know that first thing about submission or what I need. From what I've read, the BDSM lifestyle has different levels of dominant and submissive. Communication is key. If I don't know what I want how am I supposed to do this?

I take a breath. I can't leave now. I have to try, and worse that happens is I don't have to ever return. I can go live happily ever after with BOB.

My internal pep talk talk relaxes me, allowing me to enjoy the ambiance. The men working here are straight out of some supernatural romance novel, all over six feet tall, built solid and strong, just the kind of men to sweep a woman off her feet. I didn't know men like this existed outside movies and books. Maybe tonight will be a lucky night after all.

***

She's here. I felt her the moment she entered my domain. Her soul calls to mine, a lyrical melody meant only for me. I watch her as she walks to the bar, her body swaying with the sound of the music, her long auburn hair cascades down her back, and the heels I sent for her accentuate her long legs. The black lily she carries marks her as mine for all to see.

She sips the red wine so eloquently, displaying manners and grace. The thoughts flitting through her mind do not match the air of confidence she exudes, arguing with herself to stay or run. I can smell the sweet scent of her even through all the smoke and sweat of the club. My fangs ache for release, my body burns to claim what is mine.

My sweet Jasmine, a name to match her beauty.

For most of my two hundred years I have walked alone searching for the one who competes me. The one who calls to my soul, and, I opened this club in the hopes those of my kind have a safe haven to search for their soul mates.

As a species we enjoy the darker side of sex. While most of us prefer the dominant side of the relationship there are those who prefer subservient roles.

Our makers teach us the pleasures of the body, the thresholds of pain, dominance and submission. I believe it occurs naturally in us during the change, just as the need for blood occurs too, at least to the extent that we like to take things. Some of these tendencies are born in us as humans, just like those humans who chose dominate or submissive lifestyles. The change allows us to explore this natural progression. I knew none of this when I was turned long ago. These things were not spoken of, as it was not correct for socialites to discuss what happened in a bedroom. The night I turned I was taught what polite society refused to talk about. The deviant acts of pleasure that humans refused to acknowledge.

My maker was a wonderful teacher. She taught me about the body, the bliss it could behold was delightful, if not strange. I wasn't her soul mate, but she loved me in her own way and taught me for many years. She told me there was something about my soul that called to her. I was the one that would change things for our kind. I didn't believe her, I was only thirty when she turned me and new to sex, and never had a partner before her. I had no idea that pain and submission could bring about that much satisfaction. To understand exactly what someone needed to make them happy was a new experience for me. Never any fumbling around in the dark hoping to figure out what made a woman reach that pinnacle.

I was an educated man, but not a worldly one. I had no idea how to change the world for the supernatural beings, but my maker dreamed about the future, as it would come to pass, though she didn't know when. Two hundred years later, her predictions were correct, I am changing things for our kind.

Our basic sexual needs are coming to light as humans come to terms with their own wants and needs.

Yes, there are many who condemn those who seek to find release in the darker side, but it's becoming more mainstream. People are searching for pleasures untold, and this club is the playground.

It's also a hunting ground for my kind. We meet people here without persecution, safe to indulge in our sexual wants and gratifications. No one needs to know what we are. People still don't believe we exist, keeping us safe from our own hunters. We search in the city at night, but humans are only allowed in by invitation and then only on the top two floors. A select few humans are allowed in the private rooms, only when I'm aware in advance.

Most humans believe the bottom floor, the one under what is considered the basement, is storage, and that's the way I keep it.

The floor below is for our kind, vampires and other nonhuman races, to let loose and enjoy thirsts that cannot be quenched with just bondage. It is an area for more extreme play, Vampires and shifters alike tend to share blood during sex, and keeping those activities out of sight is safer. The humans are only told of our existence if we consider turning them. Not all of the humans invited are given such a choice, and those who are, have the opportunity to refuse. If they decide not to take us up on our offer, we conveniently alter their memories ensuring the safety of our secrets. It's the only way to maintain safety for ourselves and the human we seek.

I approach her, stalking across the bar and slide silently into the stool beside her and lean down to her ear. "Hello my sweet, Jasmine, I'm Marcus."

Her breath catches and she turns to me, a pink blush creeps into her cheeks. Jasmine holds out a delicate hand while the other presses to her chest trying to still her racing heart.

"Hi, it's a pleasure to finally meet you." She smiles, lowering her eyelids, a quiet giggle slipping past her ruby lips.

I kiss the hand she extends to me, her warmth radiating through my lips. "Should we move to a booth where we can talk a little more privately?" I keep her hand in mine and assist her off the bar stool as I stand. Her pulse calms, as her breathing returns to normal.

As we walk to the booth her scent wafts over me.

Pure and clean like fresh morning dew, the sunshine in my darkness. My fangs pulse for release and my cock strains against my pants. I haven't had this hard of a time controlling myself since I was a new vampire.

Jasmine calls to the animal in me to claim her, have her. The urge to throw her to the ground, taking her body and blood is almost more than I can bear. I'm not sure how long I can control myself when it comes to her.

She is perfection.

Chapter 2

Marcus. That's the name of the man who invited me. He's the most handsome man I've ever laid eyes on. Now, sitting in the booth, I have a better chance to examine him. The candle light glints off his ebony hair like the stars in a midnight sky. It curls seductively at the nape of his neck, brushing the collar of his white button down shirt. The shiny black strands sweep softly across his forehead in thick waves. My fingers ache to run through it. His eyes like the finest whiskey, amber flecked with gold, shadowed by long dark eyelashes that touch his cheeks as he peers down at me. A straight aristocratic nose highlighted by chiselled cheekbones.

My gaze is drawn to the most kissable lips, full and luscious with a perfect cupid's bow. A five o'clock shadow graces his jawline making him appear more dangerous, than the black leather pants his legs are packed in. The leather clings to him, moving like a second skin, leaving little room for imagination, as he leads me to a corner booth. His white shirt, open at the neck, revealing a smooth and perfect chest, direct from the gods themselves.

He holds my hand as we sit in the booth, rubbing his thumb across my knuckles, the electricity of his touch igniting a slow burn low in my belly. I find it hard to concentrate on mundane conversation as my clit throbs in wanton desire, begging for attention

"Jasmine? What do you do for a living?" His voice filters through the fire racing through my mind.

"I...uh... I run a homeopathic remedy store in town." I look into his eyes, losing myself in the swirling golden depths. "What about you?"

"I own this club." His eyes sparkle, pulling me deeper under his spell. "Is there any questions you have about it?"

"Yeah, I guess I do. I mean well I don't want to sound rude, but I don't get how this is so different from any other club? The people are just mingling."

"My dear this is only the social area. We don't do scenes on this floor." His laughter floats around me curling around my body, sending shivers down my spine.

"Oh, I see. What other levels are there?" I adjust my position in the booth, pressing my legs together to quell the insistent throbbing of my clit.

"There are private rooms upstairs. They are for patrons who wish to have one on one time together." He strokes the pad of his thumb over my knuckles, raising goose bumps across my flesh. "There is a lower level, playroom, with different areas set up, depending on one's fancy."

"Oh." I take another gulp of my wine, attempting to wet my own thirst.

"Tell me more about your business. Do you make all the things you sell?" He smiles.

"Yes, I do. I grow all the herbs in my garden at home.

I love making things that are good for people and safe." My heart skips a beat, at his interest in my business.

"You must be very talented to do all of that yourself."

My face heats and I know I am blushing. "Thank you. I love what I do. It's a rewarding job."

He strokes his thumb across my palm, sending electric tingles shooting through my body. Every touch he places on my hand ignites a spark in my belly. My curiosity for the other levels of the club makes my heart pound in my chest. I don't want to appear too eager, I could lose myself in a place like this. There are safety rules in place, people monitoring and watching the happenings, and safe words that must be adhered too.

Ever since he touched me the first time, my body has ached for him, a slow torturous poison swirling through my system. The lust encompasses me, like a snake coiled around me squeezing the breath from my lungs. The venom scorching through my veins, scalding my blood, Marcus is the only antidote for my passion. My nipples rub into the corset, fighting the restraint. I don't know what is wrong with me. My hormones have taken up the driver's seat in my brain, logically reasoning has not place here, lust and desire are in control.

"Would you like me to show you any of the other rooms?" The smile he flashes me tells me he knows something, but I'm not sure what.

I nod, and he leads me to the doors along the back wall.

He tilts my chin up, forcing me to meet his gaze. "Up or down?"

Knowing he means private or playroom, I decide public playroom sounds safest. I've never been into public displays, but I'm not sure I can contain myself in private. "Down."

The sounds coming from the playroom assault my ears, as we walk down the stairs. The moaning, screaming, the distinct whistle of whips being whirled through the air before the loud crack, reverberates through my bones. My heart races and adrenaline floods my system, my muscles tense, as I go into fight or flight. I don't know if I can do this. I don't even know anyone who does it.

I back up into a solid wall of muscle. His arms come around my shoulders, stroking my arms, blazing a trail of lust in their wake.

"It's okay. We are just down here so you can look around. I'll keep you safe. You don't have anything to worry about." His hot breath bathes my ear.

I know it sounds crazy, but I do feel safe in his arms, protected.

Marcus opens the door the smell of sweat and sex hit me hard, my clit throbs in time with my racing heart. My arousal seeps onto my thighs, as my core clenches in need.

Though part of me wishes I chose to go up to the private rooms to have him quench my need, curiosity gets the best of me.

He takes my hand leading me into the room. A woman is tied to a large wooden X shaped rack, naked and writhing as a man dressed in black pants teases her with a riding crop.

Her moans grow louder with each stroke he makes on her body. Angry, red welts streak across her back and thighs. I bury my face in Marcus's chest, hiding from the site as the man raises his arm to bring the crop down across her ass.

Marcus wraps his arms around me and leans down. "Look closer, listen carefully to her."

I do as he asks and notice the wetness running between her thighs, the moaning for more, in fact, she is begging for it.

We walk further into the room and my gaze is riveted to where shackles and cuffs line the wall.

People in all manners of undress are locked in the shackles. Moans drag my attention higher in the room; large birdcages hang from the ceiling with naked bodies locked inside.

"These areas are reserved for a submissive that needs to be punished." Marcus points as he continues as my guide.

My gaze continues to dart around the space. The spanking benches? I recognize those from Internet research. There are various whips, floggers and crops hanging on one of the walls. There are also various dildos and vibrators on the shelves next to them.

Drawn to the area where the spanking benches are, I curl closer to Marcus. There is a young man strapped down with shackles, his ass high in the air, covered with vicious red welts. The woman behind him holds a cane high in the air. She strikes him across his exposed ass, the skin opening up and a trickle of blood oozes down the cheek. The man is sobbing and apologizing, but it falls on deaf ears. As she brings her arm up to strike him again, Marcus turns to me.

"Stay right here Jasmine, I need to check on this." He leaves me to go to the woman in black. Marcus takes the cane from the woman's hand, her eyes sparkle with unshed tears as she runs from the room. He releases the man from the shackles and motions over the dungeon monitor. After handing the man over to the monitor He turns and stalks back to me,

"I'm sorry about that Jasmine, that woman's name is Sam, her and I have been friends along time." His eyes tell a story of sorrow. "Sometimes she gets a little out of control. I-"

I put my finger against his lips, silencing his explanation. "Marcus, that is her story to tell, if she wants me to know she can tell me."

Marcus flashes that predatory smile. "Well then love, lets continue your tour. These are the examining tables." He motions to the far corner of the room.

My heart hammers against my rib cage, threatening to break free, my breath coming in ragged gasps when I spy the medical examiner table in the corner of the room with a petite woman strapped down and her feet buckled in the stirrups.

A man flanks either side of her, one working her nipples over with a small spur like device, the other lightly flogging her spread pussy. She is begging to cum as they continue their torture of her. The sweat is glistening on her body. Her breasts rise and fall with each gasp of breath she takes. Her body trembles with the effects of the pleasure they are instilling on her. My focus is instantly drawn to the scene. The men are intensely focused on her pleasure. The outline of their erections strain against the front of their pants, the arousal they receive in bringing her to the edge of bliss evident. They find their own form of gratification in her pleading trembling body. This is an eye opener for me. There are men out there who find gratification in pleasing a woman.

I need Marcus to take me somewhere to show me why he invited me here. I pull him down to me. "I think it's time you show me the private rooms."

The expression that crosses his face is one of blatant desire, he's been waiting for me to ask. He leads me to a door in the back opposite the one we came in. He produces a key and an elevator door slides open. Ushering me inside, the touch of his hand on the small of my back blazes fire across my nerves, he pushes the number third floor button.

The butterflies are back. I'm holding his hand in a knuckle white grip. I lean into his solid frame, seeking to leach his strength into myself. No matter how nervous I am, he makes me feel safe. He smells of sandalwood and pine with a hint of leather from his clothes, I breathe him in. The scent calms my fraying nerves. He pulls me into his arms holding me close, saying nothing as we ride up on the elevator,

As the door rings our arrival, before he allows the

doors to open, he tilts my chin up till our eyes meet. "Pick a safe word."

Gasping, I know I need one, but hearing the request aloud startles me into realizing what I'm getting into. Still, I hear the word float from my lips. "Belladonna".

He ushers me into a large bedroom type room. In the far corner is a large four-poster Victorian style bed, attached to the posts are chains with padded cuffs. There's a bench at the foot of the bed with a padded seat. On the wall are different types of paddles and whips. A single chair dominates the opposite corner, at the foot of it's a large pillow. I assume for the submissive to sit there when in service. I'm new to this, having never really practiced any of it. A small dresser size stand, with four drawers, draws my eye, kicking my imagination into overdrive with racing thoughts of what is possibly contained in it. I read the consent form, marking my limits on what I'm willing to try and what I'm not right now. I know a little of what I'm getting into, but having never experienced half of what was on that paper is daunting.

The butterflies have taken up a tango in my stomach. No matter how nervous I am there is excitement too. Finally, I can live out my fantasies' see where this road leads, the mysteries it holds. All I have to do is step into this room, trusting this man to lead me into the dark and untold world he created in this club.

Marcus leads me to the foot of the bed and watches me. I try not to fidget, but his stare makes me more nervous, as the minutes tick by. "What am I supposed to do? Kneel or something?" I look up into his mesmerizing gaze.

"I need you to relax and just trust me." He walks over to the dresser, pulling a black blindfold out of the top drawer.

The site of the blindfold excites me. My breathing comes in ragged gasps, my heart hammers against my body. My arousal leaks from my slit, my wetness, I'm sure is visible dripping down my thighs. My clit pulsates a rhythm of lust. My nipples rub erotically on the corset I'm wearing further tightening the sensitive peaks. I take a deep breath and squeeze my legs together trying to quell the ache in my body. Nothing helps.

He smiles, as he approaches, like he knows how turned on I am by the sight of the blindfold. He places the blindfold across my eyes.

"Just listen to my voice, let your body feel the sensations, remember if you are scared or things are going too far you have a safe word. If you just need to slow down and take a minute say yellow and we will talk about what happened and what you are feeling." His voice, a calming anchor, in the stormy sea of emotions flooding my mind.

Then he's gone. I no longer feel him standing in front of me. There are no sounds in the room, unable to center in on his location. My heart rate returns to normal, as I relax into the darkness of the blindfold. The brush of something soft whispers across my neck, raising goose bumps along my flesh. I try to anticipate the next touch, when something icy trails along my collarbone. A shiver skates down my spine, as a hot tongue follows the cold, a whimper breaks from my throat. The tongue continues its path down my collarbone to dip seductively in the cleavage the corset displays.

My nipples, ache to be free my back arches, thrusting my breasts forward, seeking more contact. My clit throbs, begging for attention of it's own. Marcus walks me backwards until my knees bump in the edge of the bed. Laying me down, he unlaces the corset, sliding it open to reveal me to him. I'm in Heaven's arms when he takes my nipple into his mouth, grazing his teeth over the sensitive nub. Marcus raises my arms above my head I feel the cuffs lock into place around my wrists. It thrusts my breasts up like an offering to him. He continues to tongue my breasts, leaving a wet trail in the hollow between them. My pussy clenches with every nip of his teeth. He slides the satin skirt down my legs and pushes my knees apart. I try to close my legs, but he positions his body between them so I cannot. I feel the cuffs close around my ankles. A moment of panic, rushes into my system. My safe word is on my tongue. I jerk my hands, pulling violently against the restraints, trying to kick my legs, the cuff biting into my ankles.

"Jasmine, relax." Marcus's velvet voice rouses me out of my panic. He rubs my arms and legs like a scared filly. "It's okay do you need to use your safe word?"

I hear the concern in his voice and immediately begin to relax. I shake my head no to answer him.

"I need you to tell me out loud how you are feeling. Good communication is paramount for this working."

His calming tone, lulling me further into a relaxed state.

"I, uh, I'm okay," I finally stammer. It's barely a whisper, I don't even sound like myself. "I've never been restrained before. It was just a moment of uncertainty."

"Okay I am going to leave the blindfold on. I want you to concentrate on what you feel." He soothes me with his deep serene voice and once again I feel safe.

***

I can't believe how turned on she is. Her arousal, wafting around me like a summer breeze. It's taking all of my control to take this slow and not bury my cock to the hilt in her silken heat. I have to leave the blindfold on. My fangs are out and I can't force them back. I don't want to scare her already, wanting to introduce her to my sexual world, before the vampire one. She needs to know exactly what I want from her before she has to make a choice.

I take the feather, running it over her legs. She shivers and a moan breaks from her lips. I have to taste her. Leaning over I run my lips over hers in the slightest of touches. She strains against the restraints, seeking more. Happy to oblige her I slant my mouth over hers and truly taste her for the first time. I explore her mouth with my tongue savoring the exquisite flavors of red wine mingled with a sweetness that is uniquely Jasmine.

My need to great to ignore, I kiss my way down the curve of her neck, nipping the tops of her breast. I stop to graze my teeth across her nipple, taking the hardened bud in my teeth and biting. Her body arches as a moan breaks from her lips. Her breath ragged, the swell of her breasts rising and falling with each gasp. A rosy blush, flushing her olive colored skin. I lick my way down her body, centering myself between her spread legs. Her slit, glistening with arousal. I lean down licking her from the bottom of her slit all the way up around her clit. She strains against the bonds, trying to force her pussy onto my tongue. Her breath catches in her throat, her body trembles with need. I pull her clit between my teeth, rolling it around with my tongue. Her breath comes in short gasps, her body trembling with need. I pull back eliciting an unhappy groan from her lips. She furrows her brow, biting her lips, telling me she was on the edge of release.

"Please." The moan glides across her kiss swollen lips.

I run my hands up her thighs framing her glistening pussy. My fangs ache now. I lean over her body, biting on her nipple, drawing a gasp from her red lips. Jasmine strains against the cuffs, grinding her slit against my stomach. I slide down her body pulling her clit into my mouth, as I thrust two fingers into her warm wet haven. She meets me thrust for thrust, her pussy clenching on my fingers. I suck her clit, as she rides towards release. As her orgasm starts, I slide my fangs into her thigh. Her blood bursting across my tongue, searing my senses, soul, it's like finding on oasis in the desert. She is the only drink I want for the rest of eternity, pure and sweet. I pull my fangs out, licking the wounds closed as the tremors in her body subside.

I remove the cuffs from her ankles, rubbing the reddened ring, pulling her against my chest. I remove the wrist cuff, kissing the tender skin. I brush the hair from her forehead, removing the blindfold, as I cradle her in my arms.

"Marcus?" she whispers softly.

"Yes, luv?" I answer as she turns in my arms to look at me.

"I've never done that before." The redness in her cheeks, highlighting the stark blue of her eyes.

"There is a lot more we could have done, as you said yourself you are new to this, I didn't want to frighten you and wanted to give you time to determine what you want to try and where your boundaries might be." Her face gets even redder.

"No, I didn't mean the bondage part, I should have told you upfront, but I have never had an orgasm with a man before." She refuses to meet my gaze. I'm sure if I weren't a vampire I would not have heard her.

"Never before, I think, that is something we are going to have to work on, that requires we spend more time together to figure out what you like and do not like." I cup her chin in my hand, forcing her to meet my gaze. Would you like to have dinner tomorrow night? We can discuss some of things you may like to try and the things that scare you completely."

"That sounds reasonable, so you do want to see me again?" She smiles that coy smile again.

I'm lost. I never want her to leave, but I must give her time.

"I would love to see you again. Tomorrow night would be great if you can have a list started by then for us to go over."

"I can do that. What do you want me to wear tomorrow? This is the only thing I have that looks like what everyone else here wears." She waves her hand to the edge of the bed where her clothes are strewn on the floor.

I consider a moment, as much as I like her in the corset, I think casual dinner would make her more comfortable. "We can just have a casual dinner. It would be less pressure for you and give us more time to get to know one another."

Her smile, one of relief, lights up her beautiful face. "Yes that would be nice. What time do you want me to be ready?"

"I'll pick you up at eight." I help her dress and walk her to her car. "Until, tomorrow." I lean down, brushing a soft kiss across her lips, swallowing the sigh that escapes her mouth. I help her into the car watch her drive off into the night.

Back in the club, I head over to the bar. Thomas is there cleaning up from the night.

"Thomas, can you make sure everything is locked up? I am heading out."

"Yeah, I can get it. You going hunting?"

The concern in his voice making me halt my steps back out the door. "I'm going hunting, yes, why?" I level my gaze on him.

"Be careful that is all I'm saying, Mia still hasn't been located. We don't know how much this hunter cell knows about us and our location." Thomas goes back to cleaning the bar, turning his back to me.

"Damn it." I head out into the night. Thomas and Mia were friends. She was the only person Thomas ever opened up to. I knew she hadn't come back the other day, but I was too wrapped up in my own little world to pay much attention. I am definitely slacking in my duties.

I don't have to hunt to get blood; there is a supply available at the club. Being so close to my soul mate and unable to claim her has awakened the beast in me. I need the hunt, the chase, and the kill to sate it.

My feet touch down silently in the wet rundown alleyway. The air, thick with hopelessness. The syringes scattered along with the decaying trash, assaults my sensitive nose. I stop to pause, straining my hearing for signs of life. There further back in the alley, an erratic heartbeat, coupled with the stench of fear.

The man crouches in the corner of the shadowed alley, leaning against the worn down brick wall, counting his spoils. The smell of blood radiates from his hands, awaking the beast in me further. My fangs extend, I approach him, waiting until he spots me.

His face morphs into one of rage, glaring up at me. The adrenaline that floods his system smells so sweet, saliva coats my mouth.

"What they hell are you looking at buddy?" His voice full of false bravado.

I grab the grubby little man by his shirt collar jerking him up to face me, sneering I let him see my fully extended fangs. "I'm looking at my dinner."

"W...wh... what are you?"

I throw him to the ground, watching him scramble further into the darkness. He feet trying to catch purpose on the slippery wet pavement. Arms windmilling backwards, scooting uselessly into the shadowed corner.

" I suggest you run, if you want a chance at survival." The mocking laugh from my voice, bounces off the stone buildings around us.

The man runs, past me and out into the damp street. The water splashing along his legs, his goods, lying in the corner forgotten like yesterday's trash.

I give him a ten count then stalk out of the alley after him. The scent of fear and adrenaline easily marking his path. His erratic beating heart, calling me like a dinner bell. I find him curled up behind a rusty dumpster, grabbing him, I love the helpless look that crosses his pasty face. I strike, not giving him time to realize his end is upon him. The first pulse of coppery tasting life slides across my tongue, the adrenaline in his system making it all the sweeter to my beast's palate. His heartbeat falters and slows, with every deep pull I take. A whimper escapes his lips as I take one last deep drink, his body going limp in my grasp.

With my hunger sated, I take the body to the woods to

burn it, taking no chances of having some half-cocked vampire running around town. There are rules in place about the changing of humans. No kill shall be left to chance.

My feeding done for the night, I find myself hovering in the darkness outside Jasmine's house. She is stunning siting in the sheer robe, her hair pulled up exposing the sweet curve of her neck. Her brow furrowed in concentration, studying the computer screen in front of her. I peer into the window, scanning the screen in front of her; she is flitting around BDSM sites, attempting to make a list. Her fingers pausing on the mouse, to grab a pen and scribble notes. She chews the pen between her perfect pouty lips; my cock pulsates in my pants, while visions of my shaft thrusting across her lips, float through my mind.

The pull of the sunrise drags me from my obsession. I drift back to my home, vivid images of ruby red lips wrapped around my cock shuffling through my brain. . I climb into bed, letting sleep drag me under. I must rest, to continue Jasmine's instruction into total submission.

Chapter 3

Saturday morning, I'm refreshed and giddy about tonight. I don't have to open the store today. One of the perks about owning it, I don't work weekends. There are some things I need to finish before my date tonight. After pouring a cup of coffee, I stroll to the computer to finish my list from last night.

The unfinished document flashes across my screen, the crumpled papers discarded across the desk in a dishevelled pile.

I have spanking, wax play, nipple clamps, possible canes, floggers, and even more questions, than ideas, at this point. Does he want me to submit sexually or be a slave? I'm not sure I can be a slave; I don't want to give up my whole life or identity. He doesn't seem like the type of person that wants to control my whole life, but I could be wrong. I print out the list, adding a reminder at the bottom regarding questions, punishable offenses, and degrees of punishment. One final check of the list and I decide it's as good as it's going to get. I feel much better about discussing this in a more non-threatening setting over dinner though. Hopefully he feels the same about me as I do him. Last night was amazing; I've never felt such a connection to a man before. I felt so safe with him even while bound and helpless to his every desire. Thoughts about last night cause my nipples to scrape against the satin material of my nightgown. The erotic memories of his tongue laving the tightened buds flash through my mind. I need to get a grip on my sexuality if I'm going to make it through dinner. I don't know what it is about him; he has my libido in an uproar. I've never been this easily aroused before. Now, it's only a matter of thinking about Marcus and my pussy begs to be filled. I need a good, long, and cold shower if I'm going to get anything accomplished today.

Its six o'clock, he won't be here for two more hours and I can't wait to see him. The shower this morning didn't help and I've been more turned on today than ever in my life. I opt for a simple skirt tonight with a light sheer black blouse, no panty hose. I hope I can maintain some form of restraint on my wild libido, so my outfit lasts through dinner. Marcus hasn't claimed me, hell he hasn't even said he wants to keep me, but I don't want to disappoint him. I've read enough to know I'm not to make myself cum without permission. I'm not even sure that would help calm me down at this point.

Two more hours to go before he shows up. I need a distraction, pacing around the house isn't working. My skin so ultra sensitive, my nerves tingle with ever scrape of the silken material from my blouse. I'm so excited I can barely contain myself. I look in the mirror taking my hair down and fluffing the curls, again. This being the third time I've changed the hairstyle. I decide to sit down and do the store schedule for the next week, to get my mind off of the coming night, opting for mundane distractions.

The ringing doorbell shocks me out of my work. I glance at the clock. "Oh my God." I jump out of the chair, stumbling over my own feet. I lost track of time. "Just a minute!" I yell to the locked front door.

I run to the bathroom, checking my hair and straightening my blouse. Okay, still presentable. I rush to the door, swinging it open, my ability to talk lost, at the picture of perfection before me. Dressed in all black, the scent of leather and sandalwood assault my senses, my libido responds, my clit swells thundering a rhythm of lust throughout my system. My nipples perk for attention, rubbing tantalizingly against the silken fabric of my shirt. I'm lost in the mesmerizing sea of warm amber and gold. A groan escapes my lips and I squeeze my thighs together to calm the pounding beat from my clit. The warmth in his golden gaze sears to my heart, scorching an undeniable path of emotions to my soul. Love is not a strong enough word to describe the feelings that flood me.

"Would you like to come in?" I finally manage to get my brain to function enough to speak.

He smiles, that predatory gaze on his face making my body burns for him to take me. I want him to throw me to the floor in my living room and ravage me. Right here, right now. No dinner. No rules. Whatever he wants to do I'll let him as long as he takes me, slaking the fire in my body that only he has the ability to extinguish.

"We have reservations at eight. I think we should head out." The gleam in his eyes telling me, he knows exactly what I am thinking and agrees.

He is definitely trying to make sure I know what I'm getting into. I appreciate the thought from him, even if my body is way ahead of my mind.

He leads me to a limo parked at the curb of my street. Marcus opens the door, ushering me into the back seat. As he climbs in his knees brush against mine, the sparks rush from that contact straight to my clit, causing it to ripple in wanton abandon begging for him to touch it. I clutch my legs together trying to subdue the ache. He watches me intently, a knowing look on his face.

"So, have you a chance to make a list?" He breaks the silence.

It's the opening I need to get my questions out before my body overrules my brain's denial at being a slave.

"Yes, I have some questions about what you expect. I mean I get sexual submission, but do you want some total slave that you are in control of?" I can't make eye contact, afraid of the answer, but I need to know. The silence is deafening, looking up I meet his gaze.

"No, I don't want a slave. I value a woman's opinions and her independence. However, I do expect total submission sexually. Is that what you need to know?" His tone is amused. I immediately relax, comfortable with where this is going.

"Yes, that is what I need to know. It makes me feel so much better about this. I was a little afraid you would want control of everything in my life. I did a lot of reading last night and that kept making its appearance in the literature." His eyes sparkle in the dim light of the car and his smile is warm and inviting. "I wasn't sure exactly what you were looking for."

"Have you ever given total control of your pleasure over to another? Submitting to their desires and their control and just letting yourself go to enjoy the moment knowing they will take you places you've only imagined?" His voice pours over me like molten lava, my body heats in response, a low whimper slips from my mouth.

I hadn't considered the extents of pleasure a submissive received from letting go. To allow one to be free of constraints and just feel. The possibilities of that realization zip through my nervous system leaving a tingling wake of need.

"No, I didn't understand what the submissive received from this." I am trying to be as honest as possible. "I thought it was merely focused on the control and power of the dominant party, for their pleasure."

He wants open, honest communication. I am determined to give it to him. Marcus knows I am new to this, hopefully my inexperience doesn't offend him. Internet information isn't always accurate.

His smile is intoxicating as he leans over and whispers in my ear. His hot breath sending shivers down my spine.

"Would you like to delve a little deeper into submission tonight? I can take you places beyond your wildest dreams." His voice rolls across my senses, tempting me into his dark and seductive world.

My breath comes out in a ragged shallow gasp. My heart speeds up hammering inside my chest. My pussy weeps and clenches begging for him to fill it.

"Yes," I barley sigh the word as it crosses my lips. The lure of his offer too enticing to deny.

He kisses me gently with just the barest touch and my body ignites a fire burning in my loins for him to do more. I sway against him, needing the contact of our bodies. The car stops, alerting me to our arrival at the restaurant. Marcus flashes an insightful grin, as he helps me from the car. I take a deep breath as we enter the restaurant getting my libido under some semblance of control.

Marcus orders a bottle of red wine to compliment our meals at dinner. Our reservations are at a corner booth, providing privacy and a romantic ambiance.

"Do you have any other concerns you want to discuss?" He pours the wine into the glasses, sliding one across the table to me.

"I would like to talk about punishable offenses." I gulp the wine down, refusing to meet his eyes.

"What exactly do you want to know about them?"

"I need to know, I guess what you consider punishable?" I fumble with the silverware on the table to hide my shaking fingers.

"That would depend upon the type of agreement that was reached in the discussion stage." He reaches across taking my hand in his stroking his thumb across my pulse.

"The submissive has a say in it?" I look into his eyes.

"Yes, each relationship is different, so the people involved can discuss what is best for them."

"What do you consider punishable?" I lower my gaze, hiding the flaming blush creeping into my cheeks.

"I think a blatant disregard for the rules agreed upon, being unusually bratty, or even disrespectful to your partner are reasons for discipline."

"Oh. So even the rules are discussed before hand?" I raise my eyebrow in a believing stare, " I thought the dominants were in control?"

The waiter arrives with our diners, momentarily interrupting my interrogation of Marcus's lifestyle. The marinated steaks and steamed greens fill the booth with an enticing aroma. The meal is perfectly prepared, but my body refuses to focus on anything other than the way the fork disappears in his lips. The way his long elegant fingers sensually wrap around the stem of the wine glass. His rich and vibrant laugh sends tingles through my body.

"Is there anything else you would like to know, Jasmine?" He slips a spoon into the decadent desert on the table.

"I was wondering what kinds of items you use for discipline?" I stifle a moan as he feeds me bites of the dark chocolate mouse.

"It would depend on the severity of the infraction." He slips the spoon into my mouth again.

I close my eyes, savoring the creamy sweet chocolate, as it melts across my tongue, "mmm I see."

"So my sweet, are you ready to delve a little deeper tonight? His voice as rich as desert, sends a torrent of anticipation through my body.

It is the longest dinner I've ever attended. My body screams for him to take me. The light contact of our hands fan the flames of desire burning through my body. The end of dinner can't come fast enough with the question he asked echoing through my mind. Dinner comes to an end and the driver takes us to the club. Marcus leads me to a back entrance, up the elevator, to his private floor. We enter into a spacious open floor plan living room. The carpet is black and thick with sleek leather couches arranged around a stone fireplace. It's masculine and streamlined, much like the man himself. There are hints of chrome that keep the place looking modern and not too dark. The room smells of leather, my body heats in remembrance of the night before. He ushers me down the hall stopping outside of the bedroom entrance way.

"What is your safe word? Do you remember it?"

"Yes, it's belladonna." I nod to him. How can I forget anything about last night?

Smiling at my answer he leads me into the bedroom. There doesn't seem to be anything threatening in here. The bed is an antique wooden four-poster, with chocolate velvet curtains hanging around the posts, tied back with teal braided cords. The duvet, a rich coffee and the pillows complement in a soft sand tone. It's warm and inviting. Marcus leads me to stand in front of the bed, bending down he removes my shoes. The carpet is plush and soft under my feet as I curl my toes into the thickness of it. The butterflies have taken up root in my stomach again, more anticipation than nerves. Marcus starts to remove my clothes, unbuttoning my blouse, his tongue caressing each inch of skin he reveals. Patient, refusing to be rushed through anything.

My body is on fire. My slit is leaking. I can no longer contain the moans in my throat as his mouth finds my nipple through the thin lace bra. My hands rise involuntarily to his hair. God, it is soft as silk. I hold his head to my breast. Abruptly he stands, no longer touching me. The cool air surrounds my heated flesh causing a shiver to slither up my spine.

"No hands." He moves to the closet at the far side of the room, returning with a black blindfold in hand, much like the one he used before. In his other hand he also holds two sets of cuffs. He places the blindfold on my eyes and slowly peels the remaining articles of clothing from my body, stroking each area of skin that is revealed. Marcus guides me to the bed, lays me down, lifts my arms, and secures my wrists in the cuffs now attached to the headboard. The ankles are next, to be restrained. I'm completely naked and spread eagle in his bed. Last I'd seen he's still dressed. I'm utterly exposed.

***

A prefect beauty, naked on display, my sweet Jasmine, she looks like a sacrifice to a hungry God. I'm that God. My fangs are fully extended and my cock is pushing against my jeans. I lean down, running my tongue across the pulse of her neck, down to her collarbone. The moan it elicits from her is pure ecstasy. I could feast on her all night, but tonight is about her submission. Her learning to let go and the pleasures I can bring her. Taking her nipple into my mouth I lave the bud with my tongue, kneading her other breast, she tosses her head back and forth. Jasmine arches her back, pushing her nipple farther into my mouth. I pinch the other and bite down at the same time on the one in my mouth. She hisses a breath through clenched teeth as a ragged moan tumbles from her lips. I trail soft kisses down her stomach to her waiting pussy. Pain a welcome addition to her senses, she's glistening with arousal. I lick her pussy, savoring the flavor of her that is purely feminine, nectar to the gods. She thrusts her hips up trying to get me to lick her clit. Expertly avoiding what she wants the most, I nibble my way around, but never where she yearns for it.

She trembles in her craving of release. It's a magnificent sight to behold, but we need to go further than restraints tonight. Going to the dresser, I pull out a set of nipples clamps and a deerskin flogger. Tonight is about pushing her boundaries. Jasmine's breathing has returned to normal when I sit on the edge of the bed.

"I'm going to put few decorations on you now." My voice, sounding calmer than I am.

I lean over her, taking a nipple back into my mouth, I suck it into a tight little nub. Once it has tensed to attention I slip the clamp around it, sliding the edges up until she grimaces. Then loosen it just a little. I don't want her in intolerable pain, but wanting her nipples in a constant state of stimulation. The same treatment goes to the other nipple, she groans under the on slot of sensation. Her breath quickens, each ragged intake causing the twinkling of the bells on the end of the clamps. A sheen of sweat breaks out across her body, causing her to glow in the dim room light. The smell of her arousal permeates my senses. I watch as she adjusts to the new sensations, the flush of arousal creeping over her skin.

I run the flogger softly over her legs and belly, enjoying the way she trembles under the touch. Not out of fear, I would smell that. She writhes on the bed, searching for the next touch, it's a beautiful sight. I bring the flogger down harder across her thighs. She gasps, but doesn't retract from the touch. Her slit dripping with her juices. I flog her again this time across her breast. A moan breaks from her throat as she arches towards me. The twinkling of the bells and her gasping breathe the only sounds in the room. Reaching into the bedside drawer I pull out the small vibrator I place it in her pussy, turning it one and continue to flog her across her breasts. The reddened welts rising across her olive skin cause my shaft to strain against my jeans.

I strike her harder with the flogger until she is covered in welts from her breasts to the tops of her thighs. Goosebumps break out on her; she is shaking in her need. She continues to toss her head back and forth on the pillow, her pleading erratic.

I reach down and stroke her clit. Her pussy clenches on the vibrator, her moan strokes me all the way to my balls. She is on the edge. I work her clit in small circles, her body tightens as her pussy spasms on the vibrator. Her pussy gushing it's juices seeping down her thighs as she comes. I free my aching cock. Pulling the vibrator from her, I slam myself deep in her rippling passage. I bury myself balls deep in her slick hot channel, pinching her clit, sending her spiraling into another quivering orgasm.

"Oh God, Marcus, please, I need…" Her voice trailing off as I pull out and ram home again.

Her pussy brands me, coating me in her juices. Her body quakes in hunger. I jerk the nipple clamps off, pushing her breasts together, sucking the swollen buds into my mouth. She's almost there again, her pussy gripping my cock. I grasp her hips slamming into her over and over. I sit up and lean back, pulling her hips off the bed as far as the restraints allow, every thrust stroking across her g-spot.

Jasmine screams my name, the words slipping from her swollen lips in a melodic chant. Her orgasm breaks loose, her body milks my cock, ripping my own orgasm from my balls. I have no control of it. I bury my cock as far as it will go in her slick hot hole and slide my fangs into her neck, as I pump my seed into her pulsating pussy. I pull and suck her blood into me as my bite sends her into another body trembling orgasm. As she goes limp in my arms, I gently removing my fangs from her neck, licking the wounds closed. My soul aches with the need to claim her, to be with her.

I remove her blindfold and restraints, covering her with the comforter from the bed.

"I'll be right back." I tuck her gently under the covers.

She smiles in return. I slip into the bathroom to clean myself off. I return to find her sleeping peacefully in my bed. She looks at home there. Her chestnut hair contrasted against the light tan of the sheets. I gently wipe the sweat from her brow and kiss her cheek. She sighs.

I slip out the window and head silently to the damp ghetto in town. This is my favorite hunting ground, full of despair and hopelessness. They should be grateful I dispose of the waste of this city. I focus my hearing, honing in on the steady heartbeat of dinner. It won't be steady for long. I stalk off into the night, chasing my prey, the only way to sate the beast.

Chapter 4

The sunlight streaming in the half closed windows draws me from my slumber, recalling the night before I reach for Marcus, only to find the bed empty and cold. There's no impression that he has been in the bed any time recently. A little put out by the fact I've woken in a strange bed alone. I spy a piece of paper on the bedside table. After reading the hand penned note he left for me, I feel better. Being a business owner myself, I understand that things come up that need to be dealt with. I make my way to the bathroom, discovering an array of feminine bath products on the counter, with another note. My heart warms at his thoughtfulness. He picked out an array of scents, telling me to use anything that pleases me. Dare I say that I love him? Is it too soon to admit he's perfect? He is so thoughtful and caring. Yes a demanding lover, but I find myself drawn to that side of him, willing to submit to his desires. Happy with my realization, I smile to know one, but myself, I draw a hot bath and use the dark kiss bath salts and soap. It reminds me of Marcus, a mysteriously rich and heady scent.

After finishing my shower and drinking the hot coffee from the carafe in the kitchen, I head down the elevator. The driver from last night greets me, as the doors ping open.

"Good morning Miss Jasmine. Where would you like to go today?" He tips his hat smiling fully.

"I just need to go home sir. Thank you."

"No need to call me 'sir', Miss. The name's Gregory." He opens the door to the back.

I slide in smiling at the portly older gentleman. His graying hair poking sporadically out from under the driver's hat. His soft blue eyes shine with genuine warmth, behind his wire-rimmed glasses.

"Thank you Gregory, please just call me Jasmine." I settle into the limo seat for the short drive across town to my house. Only needing to go home, to work on orders and other things for my business.

After checking the voice mail messages, nothing important there, I pack the orders for shipment today. I need to post the shop schedule at the store for the week. Not knowing when I'll see Marcus again, makes my heart twinge with loss. I quickly finish my work business, feeling claustrophobic alone in my house. I think a shopping trip is in order before next weekend. I want something a little sexy and submissive just for him, wanting to surprise him, as much as he has me this weekend. My heart aches for his presence, my soul weeps for the comfort he provides, I can't believe how much I've come to crave him in such a short amount of time. I love him, the house feels too small, too confined, needing to get out, I shut the computer down and grab my purse. Heading out to the lingerie shop in town, not sure what I'm going to buy, but I have a few ideas on what I want. I wander around the shop a while until I'm captivated by the perfect ensemble. I purchase the whole set, excitement warms my cheeks.. Marcus has given me so much, allowing me to truly be myself in such a little amount of time. The least I can do, for him, is set up a surprise.

The sunlight warms my skin as I stroll along the concrete walkways. The birds are singing and the smell of just blooming flowers fills my head. Kids running and laughing match my happy mood. I turn the corner and head up the alley to my house. My footsteps echo off the tall buildings on either side. A screeching cat runs from behind the dumpster, launching my heart into my throat. The hairs on the back of my neck stand on end, swiveling around I look to see if anyone is following me. I'm alone in the alley, but that prickling feeling won't go away. I quicken my pace, never slowing down until I get inside my house and lock the door. I check all the windows and lock them too. The street outside looks peaceful and serene, but I feel something lurking out there.

After a quick dinner of sandwiches and reheated coffee, I run a bath nice and hot with vanilla bath beads. Sinking into the garden tub, I re-evaluate my feelings about the past weekend. The only word that comes to mind is amazing. I know he has only taught me a little of the lifestyle and I'm thrilled at the ability he has to play my body and my soul. Ready for him whenever he wishes, he only needs to look at me and my wetness drips onto my thighs. Just thinking about him makes my pussy clench with the need to be filled. I never thought love could hit you this fast, this hard. I'm truly in love with him and I don't want to be without him ever. I've never felt so free and powerful as I do with him. Never before did I understand the allure from Dominance and Submission. I just thought it was tying people up, the power play and the heights of pleasure to be reached didn't come to mind.

The knock at the door startles me back to reality. I wasn't expecting company. I jump out of the tub throw throwing my bathrobe on and head down the steps to the front door. I peer out the peephole; there stands Marcus in all his glory. My body heats just at the site of him. I open the door and the scent of him fills my senses, leather and sandalwood.

"Hi. Marcus. Please come in. Can I get you anything?" *Drink, directions to my bedroom?*

"Hello. Jasmine, am I interrupting anything?" He looks me up and down from top to bottom and every inch of my body awaken with hunger for him, just from a glance. I'm in trouble.

"No, I was just finishing up." I motion him inside.

We head in the living room sitting on the sofa. His leg brushes against my knee when we sit and the heat from his body through his leather pants scalds me, making me want to remove the barrier between us.

"I wanted to see you tonight. I want to see what you thought about the weekend and if you want to continue with your training?" His voice courses through my senses like a bolt of electricity. My brain ceases to form a rational thought. I'm sure he asked a question. All I can think about is running my hands over the smooth expanse of his chest, down across his flat stomach, and into the band of his pants.

"Um, Uh, Yeah…" Heat flames my face. I'm stammering now like a blubbering fool. "I really enjoyed the weekend." I manage to spit out. "I am definitely interested in learning more from you."

I want to add that part at the end just to make sure he understands that it's him, not just the lifestyle I need.

"I'm glad to hear that. Things are going to get a lot more intense for you this week. I want you to learn about servicing me and obeying my commands sexually."

"I'm willing to let you teach me, I have had a great time learning so far." I am ready for more. I want him to teach me.

"I can be demanding and rough. I need you to be sure you are ready for this."

He looks gorgeous sitting on my couch, commanding attention by his presence alone. I'm willing to fall to my knees right now and service anything he wants. I don't think it is possible for me to deny him anything.

"I'm sure, Marcus, I want to learn everything you have to teach me."

He smiles now. That dangerous one that turns my body to a pool of wanton lust, his pupils dilate with arousal. My agreement to submit to him, to learn from him, excites him. I feel powerful and sexy. This exquisite man is excited because of me.

He stands up and extends his hand to me. I take it and he pulls me to a standing position. He unties my bathrobe sliding it off my shoulder. He leans towards me I feel his breath as it brushes across my cheek. He feathers kisses on my lips, as his hands move down my arms to my wrists. He pulls my arms behind my back holding them captive in one strong hand. The other he uses to pull and twist my nipples, alternating back and forth until they are hard and sensitive.

"Are you wet for me Jasmine?" His hand slides down my ribcage, towards my waiting pussy.

"Yes."

There is no point in denying it. I'm dripping for him. I have been since I looked out the peephole and saw him standing on my porch.

He runs his fingers over my pussy lips spreading the wetness around, never touching my clit. The slow torturous exploration, causing a nagging sensation of misery to surge through my system.

He removes his hand, without fulfilling my need. I'm unable to quiet the groan of frustration that passes my lips. He smacks me right across my ass cheek.

"No complaining. You only come when I say you can. Tonight you are going to make me come."

My ass is on fire where he smacked me and the warmth radiates straight to my pussy. I can't believe how much a smack on my ass adds to my arousal.

"Yes, Marcus, whatever you wish."

"I wish for you to start calling me Sir or Master during our sexual encounters, it will keep you in the submissive role better." He flashes his devilish smile at me.

"Yes Sir." I will do anything to keep him happy. I'm too turned on to deny him anything.

"Good. Now I want you on your knees." He unzips his pants as I kneel and fists his cock at my lips. "Now take me in your mouth."

I lean forward taking his cock into my mouth. It's like velvet steel, hard, but the skin is soft. I swirl my tongue around the head and swallow him to the back of my throat. I continue to work my tongue back and forth over the ridge on the head of his cock with each pass I make. He twines his fingers through my hair, thrusting his cock into my mouth. He pushes himself into me. He takes my breath away. I try to pull back, but he holds me there by my hair.

"Don't fight me Jasmine, relax your throat and let me in."

I try to do as he says. I gag and my eyes start to water. He is fucking my mouth now, pulling my hair and pumping his cock in, out, harder, and faster.

"Just open your mouth, hold it open." He yanks hard on my hair, my scalp burning from the abuse.

I do. Tears leaking from my eyes, as he thrusts into the back of my throat. I feel his cock swell, as he pumps his seed into my mouth. I struggle to swallow it all. I'm in awe at how turned on I am right now. I have never had anyone fuck my mouth before, but for him I'm thrilled it pleased him enough to cum in my mouth. My thighs are soaked with my juices and I'm trembling with the need to come.

"Very good Jasmine, would you like to come now?"

He places his cock back in his pants.

"Yes Sir." I look up at him, the tears still leaking from my eyes, remembering what he asked me to call him. His smile tells me it pleases him I remember.

"Very well, lie back on the couch, put your hands behind your head and leave them there. If you move them, even one time, I'll stop what I'm doing. You will not come until the next time I see you, is that clear?"

"Yes Sir." I scurry to the couch and lay down placing my hands behind my head.

He positions himself between my legs running his hands down my thighs to my knees. He bends my knees spreading my legs wide. He leans over, kissing my belly button, dipping his tongue inside. Marcus licks a trail to my pussy. His hot breath floats across my soaking core. The heated flesh cools as he blows on it. Goosebumps break out along my body. He hasn't touched me yet and I'm aching worse now than before. I thrust my hips up trying to get him to touch me. Smack. Right across my pussy, I almost came right then. I feel all the blood rush to my slit, the wetness seep out of me.

"No rushing me. I'll get there when I'm ready." His voice stern, commanding.

"Yes Sir. I'm sorry. I just need. Please, Sir." I'm begging now. I know I am. I can't help it. I have never felt this desperate, this needy before.

He smiles flashing perfectly white teeth, his eyes flash an ominous amber glow. He leans down and licks my slit. I about jump off the couch, but catch myself remembering the directions. He licks me, from bottom to top. Long slow licks, avoiding my clit. I'm moaning uncontrollably now. My body trembling, I'm not sure how much more of this my body can take. He works his way to my clit. The gently kiss he places on it, not nearly enough pressure for me to come. I thrust my hips against his tongue reaching for that pinnacle that's out of reach. Smack. Right across my pussy again, that's all it took. I come shaking and screaming on the couch, the spasms rocking my body are like nothing I've ever felt before. Gasping for breath, I grab onto his forearms with my hands trying to ground myself. I'm flying, I know it. If I don't hold on I'm going to float away.

"Jasmine." He sounds serious. I look up into his face and he doesn't look pleased. "I didn't give you permission to come. As delightful it is to know pain can make you come. You didn't ask. I didn't tell you to cum. You broke the rules. There will be punishment for that infraction."

"Oh my God, Marcus I'm sorry. I didn't mean to. I couldn't stop it." I let go of his forearms, folding my arms back behind my head.

I'm trying to rationalize. I knew at dinner what would happen if I didn't follow the rules, there would be punishment for misbehavior, rewards for following orders.

"No excuses. Come here." He moves to a sitting position on the couch and pats his lap.

I know what happens now. I go willingly, accept my punishment, it will be easier, or I can fight him making it worse. I'm hoping he will go easy on me since it's my first punishment. His face, an unreadable mask.

I lay myself on his lap, opting to cooperate, still holding out hope he'll go easy on me.

"How many swats do you think you deserve?"

"Five." I stare at my carpet, shame clouding my vision. I hope he agrees to so few swats.

"I think ten sounds more reasonable. That way you will remember what punishment feels like and try harder to follow the rules." He runs his hand over my ass cheeks.

"Yes Sir." I stifle the argument in my throat. I don't want to add more to my punishment.

"You need to count them out."

The first swat lands on my right ass cheek. The heat blossoms and spreads across my ass. "One." I squirm on his lap.

The next one lands on my left cheek. "Two."

He continues to alternate cheeks as I call out numbers. "Three, four, five, six…"

My ass is on fire by the time seven comes around. My pussy is wet again. I didn't know punishment could turn me on too, by the time I get to ten my pussy is dripping. I want him to fuck me now.

"Please sir, may I come again?" I don't want to displease him twice in one night.

"No, my sweet, that is what punishment is, even though you are aroused you are not allowed to come until the next time I see you."

I think I'm going to drop dead right on the spot.

"It wouldn't be punishment if you got enjoyment out

of it, would it?" He positions me so I'm sitting on his lap facing him.

My ass chafes against the material of his pants, sending shafts of heat through me. I'll definitely be remembering this in the morning.

"No Sir." I'm unable to hide my disappointment.

"You'll get used to it my dear. You are a quick learner. I only require you to obey me sexually and never keep anything from me. Open honest communication about sex and everything else. Do you understand?"

"Yes Sir." I try to smile, but it seems forced.

I know he is teaching me how to make this work between us, which makes me happy to some degree, but my ass is on fire and my pussy is pulsing with the need to cum. He holds me close to him kissing me deeply on the mouth.

"I have to leave now." He scoots me onto the couch, gently as not to chafe my already sore ass.

My heart drops at that thought of him leaving. I wish he would stay with me, but we both have work to do in the morning. The weekend is officially over.

"Remember until we see each other again you are not allowed to make yourself cum." He kisses me again, lingering across my lips.

"Yes Sir. I'll remember." I pull my bathrobe back on and walk him to the door.

He kisses me again before stepping off the porch and heading down the sidewalk into the night. I shut and re-lock the door behind him taking my throbbing aching pussy to bed.

Chapter 5

Gregory drops me off at Marcus's private entrance just before sunset. He sent the driver to request to see me tonight. I haven't seen him in two days, and my arousal is out of control. The rub of my bra tents my nipples to hardened peaks. My clit throbs with every step as my jeans rub tantalizingly across the swollen bundle of nerves.

The dinging of the elevator opening echoes in the quiet corridor to Marcus's home. It's cloaked in shadows; the only light is the dim ray of the moon filtering through the window. I step into the doorway and just stop, unsure of where to go.

"Come in pet." Marcus's voice floats out of the darkness to slither along my spine.

The light by the end table flicks on, illuminating a sphere of carpet in front of the couch. All I can see of Marcus are leather encased legs and shiny black shoes, the rest of him remains hidden in the shadows.

I inch my way slowly into the room, my heart racing in my chest. My slit, dripping with arousal.

"Stop." His command, freezing me in place. "Strip."

I shed my clothes, with trembling fingers. I can't see his face, but his voice pours over my heated body.

"Present."

After I remove the last of my clothes, I drop to my knees in front of him. I assume the position he requests, on my knees, legs spread, hand resting on my thighs palms up. I raise my chin and lower my eyes, racking my brain to make sure this is the correct position.

The flicker in my peripheral vision alerts me to his movements. I strain to stay still and not fidget. I've learned so much from him in our time together. I enjoy the look of approval that flashes in his eyes, when I please him.

The cool leather encases my wrist, then my ankles. My body hums with delight. The thin strap he places around my neck sends a shiver down my spine. The clicking of a clasp and I feel a tug. Marcus has leashed me.

"Stand, pet, we are going to the dungeon."

I stand on trembling legs. He's never taken me to the dungeon. There are other people down there. He pulls me closer to him the scent of sandalwood and pine fills me head.

"Are you going to be a good girl?

I nod an affirmative. My voice lodged in my throat. The fire races through my system, burning a path of fear through me. I'm not ready for this.

"I need a vocal answer pet." He jerks my head upright, forcing me to meet his gaze.

"Yes." It's a raspy whisper. Sir, may I ask why we are going to the dungeon?"

"You may ask, but that doesn't mean I'll give you an

answer. I'm your Master and I choose where we play. Do you understand?"

"Yes Sir." I lower my eyes.

"Good. Let's go." Marcus heads into the elevator dragging me along behind him leashed like an animal.

The air in the elevator is oppressing, claustrophobic. My mind is racing and I can't focus. My breath coming in short ragged gasps. Oh god, I'm going to hyperventilate. My heart is skipping beats, my skin is clammy, the sweat trickles down my back, making me shiver.

Marcus pulls me up next to him. "Relax, you can do this. What are the rules?'

I take a deep breath, racking my brain trying to remember. " Don't speak unless spoken to, eyes lowered at all times, obey your commands without questions, and if things are too intense use my safe word or say red."

His smile calms me. It's the first one he has given me all night. His approval washes over me instilling a serenity that was lacking before.

The ding of our arrival draws my attention to the widening doorway. The bass from the music thrums through my core, vibrating my bones. The smell of sex and the moans of ecstasy encompass my being. The yank on the leash pulls my attention back to the present. Marcus leads me out into the dungeon, trailing behind him like a lost little puppy. He stops to talk with several patrons while he makes his way around the bar. I'm bored and feeling a little put out. I click my fingers against the D-ring on the leather cuffs, the tink tink sound giving me something to focus on.

The hard jerk on the leash causes me to tumble into Marcus's back, the scowl on his face, chilling me to my core. He has never looked at me like that before. Always the loving dominant. I don't think I like being in the club.

He leads me to the corner of the room, laying me on the medical exam table. The click of he cuffs echoes in my ears. I'm immobile besides my head. Marcus raises the stirrups, so my legs are spread wide and my feet are in the air. Anyone walking by the foot of the table can see everything I have on display.

I can look left, right, or straight up. Above my head are the punishment cages. The site sending shivers up my spine. Most the cages are empty, but two hold people inside. The two occupied ones have been lowered to four feet off the floor, so anyone walking by can poke and pinch the people inside.

Marcus moves into my line of site, blocking my vision of the offending cages, I'm lost in the amber depths of his eyes. He rubs the pads of his thumbs over my nipples, working them into tight buds. My slit clenches in need. He moves his hands to the back of my head, dropping that part of the table, my vision filled with the outline of his cock, straining against his leathers. Marcus unzips his pants, freeing his raging hard on. The slit glistening with precum.

He rubs the head over my lips and I obediently open my mouth allowing him access. He thrusts himself past my lips, to the back of my throat. I gag, gasping for breath that isn't there. He pulls out and thrusts back in. My throat burns, my eyes shed tears that leak into my hair. Marcus grabs the dampened strands and pulls my head harder onto his cock. I can't breathe.

"Relax." He twines his fingers harder into my hair, jerking my head onto his shaft. "Open your throat, let me in."

Easy for him to say, he can breathe. I grab a breath as he pulls out. The tears are streaming down my face now. I try to relax and he pushes further into my throat.

He pulls his cock from my throat and move from my line of site. Marcus leaves my head hanging down so all I can see is the wall behind me. The sharp smack of the cane across my thighs pulls a hiss from my lips.

"Damn it." I strain to get my head up to see him.

The glare I am met with stills my heart. Shit, it's the only word that comes to mind. I'm not supposed to talk.

Marcus unhooks the cuff from the table, jerking me up by my hair. I topple forward losing my balance, he pulls harder on my hair until I am upright. My scalp is screaming in denial of this abuse.

"What did you say?" He jerks my head up to gaze into his hard cold eyes.

My body shivers in fear and I retract from me, cowering. "I, uh, it slipped."

" You broke the first rule of being in the club." His anger radiates off him in waves.

Marcus drags me over to the wall, and lowers one of the unoccupied cages.

"Please, Marcus, don't do this. Please, it was an

accident." My heart skipping beats in my chest. God, not the cages.

"What did you call me?" His voice so cold and hard, like a strangers.

"I, damn it, Sir, I'm sorry." I lower my eyes, unable to stare into the frozen sea of amber any longer.

Marcus is so cold and detached it's like being with a different person. He's never been like this since we first met. He's always so loving, even if he was demanding submission. He opens the cage door and tosses me inside.

"I will be back in twenty minutes. Can you possibly figure out how to behave in that amount of time?" He turns and stalks out of the room leaving me naked with a dungeon full of strangers.

The men in the room lurk around these cages, poking and prodding the woman inside. A burly looking man saunters up to my cage. I cringe away trying to get out of reach, but there isn't any room to move. He pinches my nipples through the bars, drawing a gasp of pain from my lips.

"Do you like that slut?" He slides his beady gaze down my body.

He reaches farther in running his fat sausage fingers across my slit. My body shudders in disgust. He smiles a dirty yellow-toothed smile.

"Oh, did you like that? You are a dirty little whore." He moves closer, reaching in again, pawing at my slit.

I'm not into humiliation or name-calling, I can't take much more of this. If mister grubby is going to be here for the whole twenty minutes I'll never make it.

"Hey Steve, did you find a dirty little slut we can play with?" Man number two swaggers over, sloshing beer out of his cup.

He steps in behind the cage, pawing at my ass through the bars. Steve as his friend called him, still rubbing his hand across my slit. The man behind me sticks his finger through the cage, wiggling it around my asshole. While Stevey boy tries to jam his fat fingers in my pussy.

I can't take any more; my face is burning with embarrassment. I look around spying the dungeon monitor. "Red, red, red," I kick the side of the cage Stevey boy is on and he jumps back. The dungeon monitor runs over to my cage.

"Where is your dominant?" He looks around trying to determine who I belong to.

"Don't worry about it, I said red, now let me out of here. Find me a robe, so I can go home." I shove hard against the side of the cage wall again, making it sway on its chain.

"Okay, little lady just calm down." He shoves Steve and his friend out of the way and helps me out of the cage.

"You tell Marcus, I'm not a fucking slave and I don't play this shit." I throw the leather cuffs at the monitor and stalk out the back entrance of the bar.

"Shit." I hear muttered as I slam the door behind me. I make the limo driver take me home. I need a shower, I got grubby, dirty, man stink all over me.

Chapter 6

"Marcus?" I turn to see Anthony standing behind me. The scowl on his face sends a shiver up my spine.

"What it is Anthony?"

"Um, well sir. There has been a situation in the dungeon. Your submissive has called her safe word and fled the building." Anthony lowers his eyes.

The tumbler in my hand shatters under the force of my grip. "What do you mean?"

"Well, Steve and his buddy were groping her through the cage bars. She kicked the cage so hard it rocked on its chain and started screaming red. She fled the building after I opened the door." Anthony's voice waivers with fear. "Sir, your eyes are glowing."

I blink my eyes, taking a deep breath to rein in the beast. "Did she say anything else?"

He takes a step back from me, looking around like he is assessing his escape route. "Yes, she said to tell you she isn't a fucking slave."

"Fuck." I slam my fist into the bar top, the resounding crack reverberates up my arm. I've got to find Jasmine, she was coming along so well. Maybe, I pushed her to hard tonight, but why didn't she talk to me.

I stalk to the back of the bar, heading out to the limo driver. "Take me to Jasmine's."

He nods and opens the door. The drive is short and my nerves are burning a path of rage through my body. I can't believe she just ran out. Jasmine didn't strike me as a quitter.

The car stops and I send the driver back to the club. I beat on the front door of Jasmine's house. There is no movement inside, but I can hear the beating of her heart.

"What do you want?" She yells from behind the door, the lock never clicking out of place.

"Jasmine. Damn it. We need to talk." My voice comes out harsh.

Her breath hitches. "There is nothing to talk about. You treated me like property. You were cold and uncaring. I told you I wouldn't be a slave."

"Jasmine, if you just let me in so we can talk about this." I try to soften my anger. I'm not mad at her, just disappointed in myself for not seeing this sooner. I should never have pushed her so fast.

"Marcus, please leave. I have a lot of thinking to do tonight." Her voice cracks with her sadness. My heart breaks at being the one to cause her grief.

"Can we at least talk about this at some point?" I can't leave it like this, so close to my soul mate only to chase her away.

"At some point, maybe, I don't know yet." Her voice hitching with sobs. I hear the way her heart stutters and her breathe comes in ragged gasps.

"Alright, Jasmine. I'll leave for tonight. I'm sorry." I turn and head off into the night. Something is going to die; my beast is raging with my own heartbreak. Denying the need to break her door down and force her to submit to me, I slip into the darkened alleyway.

I hear the fluttering lone heartbeat, deep in the alley. I stalk silently through the shadows, until I am upon my prey. The grungy looking man barely eighteen, track marks line his arms. He's lining up his next hit, smacking the arm trying to find a vein he hasn't blown out. The resonating sound of flesh against flesh echoes through the heavy night air. He smells of urine and filth, I grab his shirt, dragging him to his feet. His vile breath bathes across my face. Recognition never sets in, as I try not to wretch, while sinking my fangs into his neck. The burst of tangy copper fluid slides across my tongue, tinged with the flavor of his despair. I drop his lifeless limp body to the ground.

The cell phone in my pocket rings, breaking the eerie silence of the alley. I step back into the shadows to take the call.

"Yeah," I clip.

"Marcus, we need you back at the club."

"Shit, alright Anthony I'm on my way." I lift into the air, hovering towards the club.

I touch down on the rooftop of the club. It's oddly quiet out here tonight. Nothing making any sounds at all. The owls aren't on the hunt and the cicadas are not singing. I shrug off the ominous feeling, and search for Anthony.

"What happened?" I find Anthony sitting at the bar drinking his own whiskey tumbler.

The scowl he shoots my direction raises my alarm bells. " There is a new wolf in town, She just breezed in. She shacked up in the old house just on the outskirts."

"Okay, I don't see the problem with that. New shifters are always coming here for asylum." I take the stool next to him and Thomas hands me a drink

"That's just it, she didn't come to the pack for protection. She is just holed up in her house. Hell she won't even talk to any of the shifters when she goes to town."

"Why are you so worried about it Anthony?" I turn to face him, seeing the worry lines etching across his forehead.

"Because, she is mine." His breath hisses out in a long tired sigh.

"Shit, Anthony how do you know?"

"She just got into town two days ago. The shifters have been watching her for me, scenting that she was new to town. I went out tonight to her house after you left and my wolf damn near got me to break the door down to get to her."

"Alright, calm down. You stay away from her house for a while. I will see what I can dig up after I fix my own little issue." I pat him on the shoulder and head into my room at the top of the club. Shit just got a whole lot worse around here.

Chapter 7

The light rap of knuckles on my door drags me from my exhausted slumber. "Who is it?"

"Jasmine, it's Sam. Can we talk?"

I crawl from the couch, inching my way to the door, in a shuffle of dread. She can only be here because Marcus sent her. I'm not sure I'm ready to talk about this yet.

I click the lock on the door, swinging it open, and motioning her inside. "Come in, I'll put some coffee on." I leave her in the doorway and stagger to the kitchen.

I find Sam slumped over on my couch, head in her hands. "What's up Sam? Why are you here?"

"Jasmine, Marcus is lost, without you there."

"Well if he didn't want me to leave, why would he push me away?" I hate the way my voice cracks, when I talk about this.

She levels her gaze at me, patting the sofa beside her. "Sit down Jas, we need to hash this out."

I plop down on the couch next to her, meeting her stare head on. " Sam, if he sent you here, I'm not ready to go back yet."

"He didn't send me Jas, I came because I'm his

friend, he's in a lot of pain and I just want to help. He loves you."

"Wh...what did you say?" Damn it, my voice needs to quit cracking.

"Marcus loves you. He is really beating himself up about what happened." Sam's voice soothes my broken heart.

"Why would he do that then, I don't understand?"

"Jasmine, dominants like to push a subs boundaries. It helps the submissive grow and learn. You should have talks this out with him, after you got scared, honest communication remember."

"Shit, Sam your right, but I was so hurt, he left me there. He'd been so cold all night long, I didn't understand the switch in his feelings." The hot tears stream down my face. My eyes burn with sadness and shame.

"Marcus has a hard time controlling his emotions, hon. You need to tell him this, explain how you feel." She pulls me against her rubbing my back.

I settle closer to her curling into her embrace and just cry. I don't know how to have this conversation with him, but I need to do it. Sam continues to hold me, letting me sob all over her. Shoulders shaking, my breath hiccups in my throat.

"Sam, thank you. I needed that." I pull back from her seeing her own pain etched on her face. "Sam what's wrong?"

"Jas, it's been a long week for us all." She forces a smile.

"Sam, do you want to talk about it?" Her eyes sparkles like bottomless crystal pools. My body heats, waves of lust lick at my core. Her gaze rakes across my skin, licking flames of hell fire across me. I've never been attracted to a woman before, but she is ethereal.

"I wanted to talk to you about, what you witnessed, Friday night." Her gaze flicks around the room, avoiding eye contact with me.

"I wouldn't let Marcus explain anything, it is your story, and your right to share or not." I place my hand on her leg, giving it a reassuring squeeze.

Her smile lights up her face, when she looks back at me. " I know Marcus loves you and I want you to understand, that it's not normal behavior in the club. I want us to be friends."

"I know you mean a lot to Marcus too and I would love to be friends."

"I don't like playing a dominant." She blurts out the simple statement taking me by complete surprise.

"But, you were-"

She cuts me off, " I know what you seen and it's because Marcus and I are such good friends, that newcomers assume. And also because of the outfits I wear. They don't show much skin."

I nod, not really understanding her train of thought. "If you don't like to do it why do you?"

"I can't let go and trust anyone. There are things in my past that have me scared of that kind of loss of control. Even in the safe haven of the club."

"Oh, hon. Maybe you just haven't found the right guy

yet. Don't beat yourself up, we all make mistakes." I pull her into an embrace, loving the way she molds into me. Her curves melt into mine. My body heats, and my core weeps. Damn it, I need to get a grip. I'm not attracted to woman, right?

Sam lifts her tear stained face to stare into my eyes. Her warm breath tingles across my lips. I lean in unable to stop the inevitable. Her lips yield under mine, so soft and warm. She moans quietly in my mouth. When she doesn't pull away, I lick my tongue across the seam of her lips, tasting her salty tears.

Her mouth parts, granting me access to her. I glide my tongue along side hers, she tastes of fresh summer berries. Sam hand trails up my side to cup my breast, rubbing her thumb across the nipple through my shirt. The nipple tightens to a puckered bud under her attention.

I moan, deepening the kiss. I twine my fingers through her silky golden strands, pulling her head to me. Her hands trail to the hem of my tee lifting it over my head and pushing me down on the couch. She slithers her body on top of mine. The cool leather shirt she's wearing, breaks goose bumps out across my over heated flesh.

Sam breaks the kiss, staring down at me, her pink lips swollen. "Are you sure about this Jas?"

"Yes." I can't stop now, my body is on fire. I pull her back down to me, sucking her lips between my teeth. I run my hands along the edge of her leather top, the contrast of cool leather to heated skin, a tantalizing combination.

Sam's body stills above me as I pull the leather off her body. "What's wrong Sam?"

"It's just, I haven't had my clothes off with anyone in so long. What if you're appalled?" Her body shudders.

"What do you mean? Sam your beautiful." Then I feel the welts along her back. The hardened fissures of scars. "Oh my God, Sam what happened?"

Sam tries to retreat from me. Her eyes shrouded in shame. "It happened a long time ago. Part of my past, part of the reason I can't trust anyone to submit." She yanks on the edge of her top, trying to pull it back down.

"Sam, look at me." She slowly meets my gaze. "You're beautiful."

I pull her leather top over her head, exposing her to my gaze. I lean down taking a pale pink nipple in my mouth. I suck and nip the hardened bud. Sam pushes my head hard against her chest. Her moans, music to my ears.

Her body skims down mine, her tongue dipping into my belly button. She slinks my pants down my legs, revealing me to her. Her tongue dips into the juncture of my things. My hands grasp at her silken mane. Sam buries her head in my core, her tongue licking hot fire up my slit. She thrust two of her long slim finger into my channel, curling them up to rub my g-spot. Sam sucks my clit into her mouth, rolling the bundle of nerves around with her tongue.

"Oh my God, Sam. I'm not going to last very long." My raspy breath hisses out of me in a groan.

She peers up at me over my stomach, her tongue still tickling my clit. My legs start shaking, I'm burning up. Sam works her fingers harder into me, my juices leaking onto my thighs.

"Sam." I scream as my body rides the waves of lust. I quake and tremble as she laps my cum from my core. "Oh shit, that was hot."

She grins up at me. I pull her to me, licking her lips, tasting myself on her tongue. I push her onto her back and slide over top over her.

"Jas, you don't have to-" Her sentence trails off, as I lick her dripping slit. The musky sweetness of her juices invades my mouth. Her breath hitches, grabbing her hips I thrust my tongue into her core. I savor the feminine nectar leaking out of her. Sam's ragged gasps and thrusting hips encourage my exploration. I've never done this before, but I know my way around my own. I lick up to her clit, sucking the bud into my mouth. I bite down on it. She grabs my head, forcing my face against her center, as she rides me. I slide two fingers into her slick hot channel. Her pussy clenches on my fingers, her legs tremble around my shoulder. She is so close. Sucking her clit hard, I pump my fingers faster in and out of her. With a loud groan the fluids gush from her slit, as her body shakes on the couch.

"Damn, Jas. I haven't done that in a long time." Sam pulls me up to lie beside her on the couch, wrapping her slim arms around my shoulders.

"That was fun. I've never done that." The giggle escapes my lips before I can stop it. She starts giggling.

We fall off the floor in a naked pile of arms and legs, holding our bellies, as the laughter breaks free.

"In all seriousness, could you give Marcus a call tonight?" Sam's blue eyes, sparkle with mischief.

"Oh hell, he's going to flip. I'm not supposed to be doing any of this." I wave my arms between the two of us. "Without his permission."

Sam bursts out laughing again. " Let me handle this, as you put it. You just communicate with him." She kisses me on the cheek, reaching for her clothes. "I got to head back to the club anyways. Call him Jas."

I walk her to the door, kissing her pouty pink lips. "All right, I will call him, after I have a shower.

Chapter 8

Sam storms through the club door, her body rigid. The scent of Jasmine tickles my nose. Sam stalks over to me. Smack!

"What the hell was that for?" I grab my face, damn that stings.

"How dare you treat Jasmine like that! She told you she didn't want to be a slave. You sadistic son of a bitch, you lock her in the cages." Her face flames red, her hands shake with anger. Damn she is really pissed.

"Sam, I was just pushing her boundaries, she broke the rule."

"Damn it, Marcus, she is still learning, and you, you asshole throw her in a cage. A fucking cage." Her rage boils over, she lunges at me, landing a solid punch across my face.

I grab her arms subduing her frantic swings, as she rakes her fingernails across the back of my hand. The scent of Jasmine's arousal assaults my senses. "So what have you been playing at today? I fucking smell her all over you."

Her body sags in my grip. "Marcus, I didn't mean for it to happen. I just went to talk to her. She is so loving and so caring. It's been so long since I cared about anyone. It just happened."

"Is that why you are so angry with me Sam?" I turn her to face me, ashamed by the pain I've caused the two most important women in my life.

"Marcus, please don't be angry with her. It's my fault. Her heart is so fragile. She needs you to love her, not punish her."

I pull her into a hug, crushing her to my body. " I'm not angry, Sam. I feel like a real ass right now. I'm going over there and make this right."

Sam grabs my arm as I turn to leave. "You can't go now, she is going to call you to attempt the communication part she failed last night."

"All right. But if she doesn't call soon, I'm leaving anyway." The buzzing of my cell makes Sam smirk as she turns and walks away.

"Hello." I place the phone to my ear.

"Marcus?" The hesitant voice of Jasmine pours from the speaker.

"Yes, this is Marcus. Can I help you luv?"

Her breath catches, the audible gasp heard through the phone. "Uh. Yeah, I wanted to talk to you, if you um."

"Jasmine slow down. What do you need?"

She takes a deep breath and starts again. " I would like you to come over to my house to talk." Her voice comes out in a rush.

"Okay, I will be there in fifteen minutes." I shut the phone and grab the whiskey from Thomas. I need a drink first.

I opt for dark blue denim jeans and a cotton t-shirt, I'm trying for approachable and not Dom. Sam's right I pushed to hard. Jasmine is a soft heart and she needs more affection than I gave.

I knock lightly on her front door; I hear her heart start to flutter in her chest. She opens the door, her eyes still rimmed red from crying, makes my hear sink. She motions me inside, never saying a word.

"Jasmine, please talk to me." I follow her to the couch. She motions for me to sit, taking the chair opposite me.

"Marcus." Her breath catches and her voice cracks. "I don't know if I can be what you need."

My heart breaks with her sadness. This is my fault I caused all of this. I want to take her in my arms and tell her it will be all right, but the damage may be done. "Jasmine, I'm sorry. I rushed you. Pushed you to far. Can you forgive me?"

She raises her head and stares through me with burning tear stained eyes. "Marcus, why me?"

I take a deep breath, trying to find the words to tell her how I feel, without scaring her away. "Jasmine, you're a beautiful woman, a natural submissive. Your heart calls to me, your softness, your kindness. I've done this all wrong, I love you."

The tears floating in her eyes streak down her face, her heart flutters in her chest. "Marcus, are you sure? What if I can't be what you want?"

I walk over to her, taking her soft body into my arms, kissing her gently on her tear-dampened cheek. "Jasmine, I'm sure, whatever you can be is what I need."

The small smile that graces her lips, sends a shiver of hope through my soul. She raises her ruby lips to mine, her tongue peaks out licking my lips.

"Are you positive this is what you want?" Her voice waivers with uncertainty.

"Yes." I pick her up and carry her up the stairs to her bed, laying her on the soft down comforter. I lick and nibble my way across her jawline, sucking the pulse hammering in her neck. Her body arches to meet mine. Her breath comes in ragged little gasps; her hands slide under my t-shirt.

Jasmine pushes my shirt over my head, running her hands along my chest. She raises her head, licking her way down my neck and flicks her tongue across my nipple. The groan that escapes from my lips, sneaks a smile across her face,

"Make love to me Marcus, because you love me, not as Dominant and submissive, as lovers." She wraps her legs around my waist grinding her body against my erection.

I peel the shirt from her body, exposing her hardened nipples to my gaze. The rosy flush creeps along her chest and up to her cheeks. I slink down her body, trailing my hands along the curve of her hips, sliding her pants off her legs. Once she is completely naked, I remove my own pants. I sit on the end of the bed between her spread legs, lifting her foot to my mouth; I kiss the inside of her ankle.

The goose bumps break out along her leg. She gazes at me with need and love in her eyes. I trail soft wet kisses to the juncture of her thighs. As I blow cool air across her heated core, she twines her hands in my hair.

She arches her body, pulling my head to her center.

I lick her slit, savoring the sweet flavor of my love. Her grip tightens on my hair pulling me hard against her. I suck her clit into my mouth and roll the bundle of nerves with my tongue. Her arousal leaks onto my chin. She grinds herself against me.

"Don't hold back Jasmine. Let me hear you. Let yourself go."

Her breathing becomes short and shallow. " Oh God Marcus, please-" Her voice trails off in a ragged groan as her body drops over the edge into orgasm. Her legs tremble and shake, as she rides the waves of ecstasy.

I move up her body, kissing my way across her face, to capture her lips, thrusting my tongue into her warm wet mouth. She sucks my tongue, biting at my lip. Her body arches as she rubs her wetness along my shaft. I inch into her tight slick channel, savoring the way it hugs my cock. Her body stretches to accommodate me.

"Please, Marcus." Her whimpers, driving me on.

I pull out of her warm wet haven and plunge in again. Her nails score down my back, as she raises her hips meeting me thrust for thrust. Her pussy sucks and clenches around my cock, bringing me to the brink of insanity.

"Marcus, please, I need-." Her head thrashes on the pillow, her body rigid and strung tight.

I grab her hips plunging into her harder and faster. Her body quakes with need, she buries her head in my shoulder. As her orgasm over takes her she bites into my neck. Unable to control my self any longer, I slip my fangs into her neck, as my cock pumps my seed deep into her body. Her blood burst across my tongue, her body soars into another trembling wave of ecstasy. I slide my fangs from her neck licking the wounds closed as her body goes limp in my arms.

"Jasmine?" I brush her sweat caked hair from her face.

"Hmmmm?"

"I love you."

She never opens her eyes, half asleep in my arms, she murmurs, "Marcus, I love you too."

Chapter 9

The sunlight, streaming though the windows, awakens me from my perfect dream. My body sore, in the most pleasing of ways. The bed is empty where Marcus had been when I drifted off. The hand penned note on the stand, the only visual reminder of his visit.

With a light heart, I shower and head to the shop for the morning rush. The birds seem louder, the air clearer, than ever before. I'm a walking cliché, basking in the loving after glow of Marcus.

The shop is only a short walk from my home. Putting the key in the door, I start the morning checklist. Lotions are going to need to be made to restock this week. The dried herbs need refilled; I can take those out of storage at home. There are a few notes left for schedule changes on my desk and a few personalized orders I need to fill.

I check the cash box and turn on the store lights at nine, unlocking the door to await the string of customers.

The dinging bell over the door draws my attention to a cute little old lady, bent over walking with a cane. She smiles up at me.

"Would you have anything for arthritis in here my dear?" She rubs her fingers together. The knobby joints swollen.

"Yeah there are some teas over hear that might help you." I take her hand leading her over to the far counter.

I pick out three different flavors. "This is stinging nettle tea, it can help with pain and ease inflammation in the joints. Usual dose is three cups a day." I hand her the packet of tea.

"What are the others?" She puts the tea in her purse.

"These are Devil's Claw and this one is Ginger Root. Why don't you take samples of all three of them home? You can come back if one of them helps." I put the rest of the teas in her hand.

She pats my arm, smiling. "You are such a nice girl."

The door dings again and two men walk in, behind them a few more women. The women heads over to the beauty creams and lotions. The men just wonder about. That prickling sensation from the other night creeps up my spine, raising the hairs on my neck. I look around, but no one is watching me. I help the little old lady walk to the door, holding it open for her.

The woman are talking and sniffing the different lotions. I head over to see what kinds they want this week. I stroll past one of them men and he bumps into me.

"Excuse me." I turn towards him.

"Oh, yes, excuse me miss." He has a cruel smile. His beady eyes rake over my body, sending shivers skirting up my spine.

I back away from him, going over to help the woman. The shift girl should be here soon. I occupy myself with the woman chatting about the different uses for each lotion and tonic.

That prickling sensation won't go away, glancing up, Mr. Beady Eyes is still staring at me. He isn't even trying to not be obvious. The man with him taps him and the shoulder and nods. They both leave the shop and the breath I didn't realize I was holding rushes out. That was creepy.

The shop girl comes in around noon; she's on a work-study program from school. I leave her to run the front of the shop and go back into the office to fill the Internet orders and make a list of supplies for the personal orders.

We close the shop at five, the sun still shining on the treetops outside. I lock the door behind me, taking my lists and walking towards home. There aren't many people out now, most have already headed inside for dinner this evening or out on the highway fighting rush hour traffic to get home. I don't even own a car; my shop is within walking distance to home, even in the winter.

The hair on the back of my neck stands on end and my stomach flutters with nervousness. The alley to my house shadowed in darkness. It's never bothered me before walking home this way; those men must have really messed with my senses tonight. My footsteps echo off the buildings, ringing an alarming warning in my system, quickening my pace. A screeching cat leaps from behind the dumpster, squealing I leap against the building. I take a deep breath and assess my surroundings. I'm alone.

I continue my short walk home, breathing deep, trying to calm my nerves. The front light to my house in on, highlighting a box on the porch. I skip up the steps; it's a flower box. I pick it up and quickly get inside the house. There can only be one person to send me flowers.

I lock the front door and put the box on the table. I open the red wine bottle to let it breath and tear the pretty red bow from the box. The most beautiful Madagascar Jasmine blooms I've ever seen in the box. I search for a card, expecting the familiar handwriting of Marcus. The card bears no signature, just and unknown scribble saying, *See you soon.*

I toss the box into the trash and check to make sure the windows and doors are locked. This is crazy I've never in my life had anything like this happen. Why now? I wonder to myself if it has anything to do with Marcus or his club.

The only thing strange that has happened in our little town is the unexplained animal attack across town. They found some homeless junky with his throat ripped out. Maybe it wasn't an animal; maybe it's a serial killer. I'm not a homeless junky though, so why would I be targeted. I grab the wine bottle off the counter and one glass, heading to the bathroom. I'm sinking into the hot bubbles and not worrying about this right now. It was just a creepy guy; I'm not stalker bait.

Chapter 10

I hover outside her window, just watching her lithe body, swaying to the music in her room. Her auburn hair swirls in seductive waves, as she twirls. Her robe half open reveals the gentle curves of her body. My cock hardens at the site of her pert dusky nipples. Her olive skin glistening in the moonlight.

I land softly on her porch, wrapping my knuckles against the font door. Jasmine swing the door open, her eyes shine with desire.

"Marcus." She motions me insides, her heart fluttering.

"How was work today?" I pull her into my lap on the couch.

"It was okay. I missed you." She nuzzles her lips into my neck.

I run my fingers along her thigh, resting it on the curve of her hip. "Jasmine, my love, we need to talk a little more."

She sighs, her hot breath whooshing over my skin. "I know, I've been doing some more research so I can have a better idea of what I don't like."

"Well then why don't you tell me what you want out of submission?" I stroke the soft swell of her belly, trailing my hand up to thumb her nipple.

"Marcus, I can't think with you doing that." She pushes my hand down to rest on her thigh and smiles. "Okay, now I definitely do not like the cages, I don't like to feel abandoned and like property."

"I know Jasmine, I'm sorry about that. I knew how much the cages scared you."

"Marcus, it's all right we are past that now. I don't like the leash around my neck, it was so cold and detached from you." Her voice cracks as tears form in her eyes.

"My love, don't cry. I never meant to hurt you." I pull her head into my shoulder, stroking my hands along her spine.

"The single tail whip, the sound it makes scares me." She shudders in my arms.

"What about anal or other people?"

She stiffens in my lap, her heart rate ratchets up another notch. "I've never done anal, so I don't know about that."

"What about other people Jasmine?" I can't keep the smile out of my voice.

She looks up at me, a blush creeping up her cheeks. " You know about Sam?"

"Yes, I know about Sam, did you enjoy it?"

Her face flames a deep red and she bites her bottom lip. " I did." She diverts her gaze from my face.

I grasp her chin tilting her face to look at me again. "Don't be embarrassed with me Jasmine, not about anything." I lean in licking the seam of her lips, swallowing the moan that escapes her mouth.

She wraps her legs around my waist, twisting her fingers into my hair. She thrusts her tongue in my mouth, the heat of her sex scorching my cock.

I trail my hands down her back, sliding them under her robe to cup her ass. She groans against my mouth, licking her way across my jaw to nip at my neck.

The scent of her arousal encompasses me, enveloping me in the intoxicating aroma of Jasmine. Her wetness seeping into my jeans. I push her down on the couch, hovering over her body. I trail my fingers lightly across her swollen sex, spreading the wetness around, bringing the glistening digit to my lips, savoring her juices.

Her lust filled gaze watching my every move, leaning down I lick her slit. Her body jerks against my mouth. I wrap my arms around her hips pinning her in place. I nibble my way down her slit, raising her hips up, I tongue her puckered virgin hole. Her moan strokes my soul.

"Mmmmm." She thrusts her hips hard against my tongue.

"Do you like that luv?"

"Yes," she breathes out on a ragged groan.

Her pussy is leaking her juices out, coating her thighs, running down her crack. I coat my finger in her wetness, sliding it into her ass. I suck her clit into my mouth, biting down on it. She is riding my finger, thrusting herself up and down. I push a second finger into her, feeling her muscles relax and open.

"Marcus, please," she groans.

I remove my fingers from her ass and free my raging

hard on. I ram my cock into her dripping pussy. I slam into her again and again, using her hips to hold her to me. Her body draws tight. Her slick hot channel pulses around my cock, sucking my orgasm from me. I slam myself deep in her pussy, groaning out my own pleasure.

I kiss her cheek, pulling her back into my lap. The sexual after glow on her skin, radiates like moonbeams through a darkened night sky. Her breathing in short shallow gasps, her hair dampened with sweat. She is never more beautiful.

Jasmine gets a serious expression on her face. "Marcus, have you been reading the paper? They found some homeless guy attacked by an animal across town."

My heart skips a beat in my chest, shit I forgot to dispose of him. "Uh, no I hadn't heard. What's the matter?"

"Well the paper said they thought maybe it was a serial killer or something." She wraps her arms around my neck, burying her head.

"What happened today that you are worrying about serial killer?" I stroke her back, her body shaking in my lap.

"There was a couple creepy guys at the shop today and when I got home there were flowers on the porch, I assumed from you." She shivers and takes a deep breath. "The card said 'see you soon', that was it."

"Jasmine, you will be okay, I won't let anything happen to you. Why don't you come stay with me tonight?"

"I would like that." She kisses me and gets up.

"I will call the driver, you go pack." I swat her ass sending her skipping to her room.

Chapter 11

It's dark outside when I awake, alone in Marcus's room. The shades drawn, the clock on the end table read eight o'clock. I get up and slide into jeans and a tank top, taking the elevator down to the club level. I've not been down here since I ran out.

The ominous ding of the doors opening, sets my nerves on edge. The music isn't on yet, the bar looks innocently inviting. Spying Marcus at the bar with Sam and Thomas, I head that way.

Marcus turns to me as I approach them, his eyes flash a glowing amber, before it's gone. I shake my head, clearing the fog from it. I must still be half asleep; people's eyes don't glow. The warm smile that graces his handsome face beckons me to him. I lean into him, kissing him. His arms slide around my waist pulling me against the hard planes of his body.

"Did you sleep well my luv?" Marcus pulls me into his lap.

"I did. Are you guys setting up to open the club tonight?" I settle onto his lap wrapping my arms around his neck.

"We are, we were also discussing your scare about the serial killer in town."

Marcus eyes Sam and Thomas, they both have unreadable expressions on their faces. Thomas starts wiping down the bar top again and Sam downs her shot.

"Do you guys know something I don't?" I look back and forth between those two.

Sam chokes on her drink, wiping the dribble from her chin. "No Jas, we haven't figured out anything yet. Marcus was telling us about the strange flowers you got."

"I didn't expect them to be from anyone, but Marcus. It was definitely stalker type material. I just haven't figured out why I would be a target." I lay my head on Marcus's shoulder.

They all exchange that knowing glance again. I feel like I'm the only one missing part of the story here. I swear Sam's eyes just flashed, maybe it's a play on the lighting in here or I'm not awake enough yet. I slide off Marcus's lap, turning to kiss him.

"I think I am still tired. I'm going back up to the room, are you coming?" I slide my body against his purring in his ear.

He grabs my waist pulling me hard against him. "I will be up in ten minutes, hope you aren't that tired."

My body heats at the suggestion, I exaggerate the sway of my hips as I stroll to the elevator. His laughter floating around me cloaking me in warmth and love.

Back in the room, I strip out of my clothes, and lay in the middle of the bed. I relax into the quiet of the room, letting the worries of stalkers flee from my brain. The duvet on the bed, a soft brushed velvet, tickles against my skin. I trail my hands along my body, the nerves ultra sensitive to my touch. My skin breaks out in goose bumps and my nipples harden. I slide my hand between my legs, my slit dripping with my arousal. I cup my hand over myself, pushing the palm of my hand onto my clit, trying to easy the ache.

"What are you doing?"

Marcus's stern voice jolts me from my lust filled haze. I jerk my hand from my self, laying it beside me on the bed.

"I, uh, um." I open my eyes, unable to form a coherent sentence.

"Are you too eager to wait for me?' He lifts my hand, sucking my fingers into his mouth.

The lust in my body blazes from my fingertips to my clit, making it throb in want. I stifle the moan threatening to break free.

"Jasmine, don't hide from me, I want to hear you." Marcus leans down and nips my ear lobe.

"Mmmm." The ragged groan slips past my lips.

"I want to take you back down to the club tonight." He flicks his tongue along my neck.

"Are you sure?" I shudder under his attention.

"Yes luv, but I just want you to watch. We won't play tonight. I want you to get more comfortable in that setting." Marcus nips his way across my jaw, licking at the seam of my lips.

I obediently open granting him access. He thrusts his tongue inside, consuming me. His hands trail up my sides, to rest under the curve of my breast. The air in my lungs freezes, waiting for his next move. He ends the kiss, rising from the bed. My breath hisses out in disappointment.

"Come on luv, let's get you ready." He pulls me to stand beside the bed. "Stay right here."

Marcus walks over the closet, pulling out an array of items. Some I recognize, some I have no idea what they are for. My heart palpitates in my chest, with anticipation. He tosses a handful of items on he bed. He slants his mouth across mine, winding his fingers in my hair. My nipples pucker into tight buds and my slit drips, responding to his touch.

His thumbs rub across my already sensitive nipples, something cold and hard slides over the end of one. The ensuing pinch, dragging a gasp from my mouth. The sensation of constant pressure trails fire though my body. He tugs at the clamp he place, I sway towards him, my eyes flutter closed. He slides a clamp around my other nipple. My body shudders with desire.

"Do you like that luv?"

"Yes Sir." My body blazes with arousal. My voice takes on a husky lilt.

Marcus runs his fingers through the wetness at my core, a pleased expression on his face. He turns me around leaning me on the bed, face down, ass up. The cool lube against my heated ass sends a shiver slithering up my spine. He pushes his finger into my ass, working it in and out past the tight ring of muscles.

"Relax luv. Deep breath."

I take a deep breath, as the hard plastic tip of

something presses against my ass. The broad enters me and my nerves fire off a rapid succession of lust through my body. I'm stuffed full, the plastic toy fully seated in my ass. Marcus stands me back up, with a dangerous glint in his eyes. He holds a black box in front of my face, clicking a button. The vibrations rush though my body from my ass to my clit, my muscles pulse around the toy. My legs go weak; I tremble and tumble back onto the bed.

"Oh my God, Marcus."

His laughter swirls through the room. "Do you like that?"

"Marcus that is cheating." I attempt to gain control of my legs to stand up.

He kisses me hard on the mouth, clicking the vibrations off in my ass. "Lets go to the club." He grabs my hand and leads me to the elevator, holding me close to him the entire ride down.

The music is thumping now and the room is packed with people. We go over to one of the booths and he pulls me to sit on his lap, toying with the nipple clamps.

Sam comes and sits with us, her gaze focused on the golden bells dangling from my nipples. She licks her lips and her blue eyes darken with lust.

"Aren't they pretty Sam?" Marcus flicks the bells.

"Very nice Marcus, she looks lovely all dressed up."

He slides me off of his lap onto the booth beside him. "I'm going to go get some drinks, I will be back in a little while." He winks at Sam. "You girls have fun."

"Oh we definitely will." Sam winks at him, reaching

across and tugging the clamp.

Sam gets up and sits in the booth next to me. Her dark gaze fixated on my tits. She pushes me back against the wall, her tongue flicking out to lave my hardened nipples. My fingers twine through her hair, pulling her hard against me.

"Sam," I hiss through pursed lips.

Her hands slip down my sides, resting at the juncture of my thighs. She pushes my legs as far apart at the seat allows. Her fingers trail through my wetness, coming to rest of the base of the plug in my ass.

"What do we have hear?" She taps the plug, sending ripples of need through me.

"Uh, Marcus thought it would be fun." As I finish the sentence the vibrations kick on. I cling to Sam's arm, to ground the waves coursing want through my ass.

"Oh isn't that interesting." She dips her fingers into my core, rubbing up against my g-spot.

"Oh God, Sam." My nails bite into her arms.

Marcus returns with the drinks, an evil grin on his face. The vibrations cease. Sam removes her fingers from me and takes her seat on the other side of the booth.

Marcus slides in beside me, handing me a glass of wine. "You look like you could use a drink luv."

A drink, hell I could use a vat of ice water right now. I'm never going to make it through the night with these two. I take the glass and gulp the wine down, in an attempt to quench the ache.

"We should take her over to the stage to watch the

performance tonight." Sam's devilish grin, doing nothing to quell the ache I have now.

"That's a lovely idea Sam." Marcus takes my hand and pulls me out of the booth. My body molds to his as he brings his lips to mine.

He leads me over to a stage at the edge of the dance floor. He sits in the front row, settling me across his lap. He faces me sideways with my legs dangling over one side of his lap he turns my chin to look at the stage. Sam sits in the chair behind me.

There is one woman on the stage, tied to a bed. The spotlight on her shadows the rest of the area. Her breasts rising and falling with each gasping breath. The pale skin of her thighs lined with thin red welts. A man stalks form the corner of the shadows, whooshing a cane back and forth. The woman's breath hisses out of her mouth as he connects the cane across her legs. Her slit glistens in the lights.

My arousal leaks onto Marcus's lap. His hard cock pressing into my ass. I squirm on him trying to ease my aching clit. Marcus leans forward running his tongue over my shoulder, just as the vibrations in my ass start again.

"Ooh." My head falls back and my eyes fluttered closed.

"Watch the show luv." Marcus raises my head back up turning me towards the stage.

I watch through half lidded eyes, unable to concentrate on the show. My clit pulsating with every wave of vibration that passes through my ass.

The vibrations stop and I take a deep breath, trying to relax. The woman on the stage is pleading with the man, as he thrusts his fingers into her pussy. Her juices run down her thighs. The man smacks her swollen pussy and she comes quaking and screaming. He continues to rub her clit, sending her careening into another ear piercing orgasm.

"Do you think you would like to do that?" Marcus nips my shoulder drawing my attention back to him.

"If it would please you, I will try."

"Come on girls, I think it's time to head back upstairs." He picks me up and motions for Sam to follow.

Marcus holds me all the way up to the room. I'm having a hard to focusing, my mind racing a mile a minute. Girls, he said, Sam is coming up with us. I've no idea what to expect to happen. Am I ready for something like this? I've been with Sam and Marcus separately but I've never done anything like this.

Marcus lays me in the center of the bed and Sam climbs in on my right, She curls her body up against mine. The cool leather of her outfit brushing against my skin. The bed dips as Marcus climbs in on my left.

"Are you okay luv?" He strokes his hand along my thigh.

"I think so, I've never, um, this is new." I shudder as Sam's tongue flicks across my nipple.

"We don't have to do this if you don't want to." Sam turns my head to look at her. I see the loneliness swimming in her clear blue eyes.

"It's okay, I uh, I don't mind." My body breaks out in goose bumps, as Marcus turns the vibrations on in my ass again.

Marcus pulls the satin blindfold out of the nightstand. "Tonight, I just want you to feel." He wraps the fabric around my eyes.

I sink into the darkness, every other sense heightened. The sweet smell of Sam's perfume tickles my nose. The warm lick of a tongue on my left ear. A gentle brush of a hand on my clit. My hips jerk up seeking more contact. The soft chuckle that pours from Marcus.

"Roll over luv and spread your legs." His voice full of demand.

I abide his command, lying on my stomach with my legs spread. A hand blazes a trail of want down my back, tapping on the vibrating plug. Two fingers dip into my dripping core.

"Oh God." My legs tremble and my belly flutters.

A tug on my hair raises my head from the bed, legs come around my shoulders. Marcus inches his cock into my slick channel. It stuffs me full with the vibrating plug still in my ass. The nerves in my ass and pussy fire off in tandem driving me to the edge.

"Not yet luv." Marcus pulls out of my channel and slides back in.

Marcus pushes my head forward, the scent of Sam's arousal filling my nose. Her wetness coats my lips, sticking out my tongue I lap at her core. Her legs shake by my head, hands twine in my hair pulling me harder against her. Marcus pumps in and out of my pussy. The vibrating plug set on a pulsate rhythm sending waves of sensation through my ass.

"No coming luv, not until Sam get's there first," Marcus whispers behind me.

I'm right on the edge, ready to barrel into bliss. I suck her clit into my mouth, biting the hardened nub. Her breath comes out in pants, tickling the hair on my face. Her legs squeeze my shoulder, as her body tightens towards her release. She yanks hard on my hair grinding into me, as her wetness coats my face. A moan breaks from her throat as her legs quake with ecstasy.

"Good girl. Come for me Jasmine." Marcus jabs his cock hard into my dripping pussy.

"Oh fuck." My body drops over the edge of the cliff.

Sweat trickles down my forehead, as the waves of orgasm rack my body. My pussy clenching and sucking on his cock. My ass gripping onto the plug. Marcus's fingers bite into my hips, slamming me hard against him. His cock swells, pumping his hot come deep in my core.

Marcus slides out of me and removes the plug, my body clenches at the empty feeling. Sam slips from under my head. Someone removes the blindfold, I stare up into loving amber eyes. His smile warm and inviting. I reach for him, kissing him with all the love I feel. Then I turn and snuggle into the pillow on the bed, as exhaustion claims me.

Chapter 12

Sam and I stalk out of the club to the ghetto side of town. Sam won't let me go hunting alone since I left the body last week. We land silently in the dark alley I've claimed as my hunting ground. The rain, stirs up the smell of death and decay. The sopping wet trash, remnants of yesterday, laying discarded with the baggies and needles. The junkies still hang out in this alley even after the dead body of one of their own was found, nothing deterring them from getting that next high.

There are two quick heartbeats fluttering in the shadows. I motion Sam to follow me. The sounds of flesh slapping and moans assault my ears as we walk closer. The sight of the bone skinny woman pressed against the crumbling brick building, with her dealer pounding into her, sickens me. Have these people no sense of shame, of self worth. Selling everything they are, or have, for five minutes of high.

"You take the girl, I want the dealer." I turn to Sam her blue eyes glowing with the same rage I feel.

She nods, stalking further into the shadows. I walk into the dim light filtering through the cracked and stained windows. The dealer turns to face me, his blissful face morphing into one of rage.

Sam leaps out of the shadows and grabs the woman from the wall, jerking her off the dealers prick. I lunge slamming his body into the wall that is now empty. Sam's fangs slide seamlessly into the sluts neck, silencing her utter of surprise. I gouge the man in the throat ripping away chunks of flesh, tearing into the soft skin of his neck. His cries gurgle out of his throat, while his quickening heart pumps his blood faster into my mouth. His tastes of sin, death, and despair. The warm coppery blood slips down my throat sating the beast within.

"Geez Marcus, messy much." Sam drags the lifeless hooker through the stagnant mud puddles.

"Damn it Sam, I can't keep going on like this, being this close to Jasmine and not having her is driving me mad." I grab dealer man by his shirt dragging him behind me.

"Let's dump these bodies, then go check out that new girl in town. The one that has Anthony in an uproar." She leaps into the air, effortlessly hauling up her prey.

We burn the bodies out in the woods next to the edge of the pack lands. Heading back into town we stalk around the house of the new girl. The house is run down, with an old clunker car parked out front. There are sheets hanging on the windows, acting as curtains. The slim silhouette of a woman passes by the windows, walking from room to room.

"Smells like a shifter, wolf I'm betting." I turn to see Sam's eyes flash in the darkness.

"Something is off Marcus."

"What do you men off, I don't smell different, but her." I turn scenting the air, still nothing.

"The adrenaline pumping off of her isn't normal. Something is off with her."

"Well maybe you and Jasmine can come out this week and say hi. Get to know her, see if she will let you two in."

"Come on Marcus the sun will be up soon. We need to head back, and you need to figure out how to claim your woman." She punches me in the arm and vaults into the air, leaving me standing alone in the shadows.

I jump into the air leaving the scent of wolf behind. I need to get my own love life under control before I try to help anyone else.

Chapter 13

"Wake up, Jas." Sam shakes me rousing me from my slumber.

"What could you possibly want already?" I pull away from her covering my head with the pillow.

"Already? Girl it's the next night, you slept all day." She pulls the pillow off my head, smacking me with it. "Now get up and get a shower, there is someplace we need to go. Fill you in on the way." She yanks the comforter off the bed on her way out of the room.

"Bitch!" I throw the pillow at the door. Her laughter echoes down the hallway.

I drag myself out of the bed, stumbling to the shower. "There better be coffee when I am done woman."

Sam laughs, but I hear clinking in the kitchen, as I turn on the shower tap. The hot water soothes my achy body. God, I am sore in places I didn't know could be sore. I soap up and rinse off, finishing up my shower. I opt for jeans, boots and a black tee, nothing fancy I don't know what she has planned.

I stomp my way to the kitchen, I never used to sleep the day away. These people are draining the life out of me. As I round the corner into the kitchen, Sam hands me a cup of steaming coffee. I give her a half smile, inhaling the rich aroma.

"So, what do you have up your sleeve today?" I sip the hot black liquid energy I'm going to need every once of it tonight.

"There's a new girl in town, I thought we could pop into your shop, grab so welcome stuff and go say hi." She hops up on the kitchen counter, swinging her feet like a giddy kid.

"So we are going to show up at some woman's house and invite ourselves in?"

"That's the plan."

"All right, lets get going." I pour the coffee into a travel mug and drag Sam off the counter.

The shops closed, so we head in the back door. I grab a basket and Sam heads out front going through products. I step into the office, to check messages from the girls working. There's a white flower box sitting on my desk. It's the same kind of box that I found on my porch that day.

"Sam!" I jerk the lid off the box.

The same white flowers are on the inside. The same-penned note, it's the exact handwriting from before. Sam rushes into the office door. She stops and stares.

"What's that?" She pulls the card from my hand.

"Sam, I don't know who keeps sending these. It's really starting to creep me out." I chuck the flowers in the trash, with trembling hands.

Sam pulls out her cell, typing in a few quick text messages. "Come on, let's get this basket together and get out of here. Do you have the schedule for the store covered through the end of the weekend?"

"Yeah, I do. I don't have to come in at all, except Sunday to restock and post the new schedule." I grab the basket, tossing in all the things Sam grabbed.

The limo drops us off, about a block from the house we are going to. Sam doesn't want to appear uppity to this woman. She promises to call him as soon as we are ready to go back.

"Okay lets do this." She pulls me up on the porch, knocking on the door before I can protest.

The clicking of locks, two of them, and the rattle of a chain, precede the opening door. A tall slim built woman with pale blonde hair stands in the doorway. Her eyes dart to the street behind us, before leveling on the basket in my hands.

"Can I help you?"

"Hi, I'm Jasmine. This is Sam." I motion to my now silent partner. "We just wanted to stop by and welcome you to town."

"I'm Allya." She blocks the doorway with her body.

This isn't going too smoothly.

"I made this house warming gift for you." I thrust the basket into her arms.

She sniffs at the contents. "Uh, thanks. Do you want to come in?"

"Sure." Sam grabs my arm and pushes past the woman.

Allya huffs under hear breath, something about fires, I think.

"Have a seat ladies." Allya motions to the worn couch in the living room. "Do you want something to drink?

I've water, tea, and there might be some wine left."

"Sure, wine sounds great. I'll help you." Sam follows Allya into the kitchen, leaving me in the living room.

There is mumbled conversation going on in the other room. I strain to hear, only making out a few words. An okay, and an oh I see. There is the clinking of glasses then they appear in the doorway carrying a bottle of red wine, three glasses and a plate of fruit and cheese. Guess we are making an evening of it.

"So since you guys are the welcoming committee. What is there to do in this town?" Allya takes the seat opposite the couch, placing the wine on the coffee table.

"Well we go to the Black Lily a lot." Sam places the cheese tray down and smirks as she sits beside me.

"Yeah there is the club, I run a shop in town too if you're looking for work." I pour the wine into the three glasses on the table.

"What kind of club is it?" Allya takes one of the wine glasses, sipping at it.

"It's a sex club." Sam pops a cheese cube in her mouth, hiding her grin.

"A what?" Allya chokes on her wine.

"It's an alternative lifestyle club, BDSM." I elbow Sam, to get her to stop laughing.

"I see." Allya bursts out laughing.

"You two are hopeless," I sigh.

They break out into a giggling fit; I can't help but to laugh along with them. It's kind of nice to have some girl friends.

"Allya, would you like to come by the shop

sometime. It's not hard work, but it's local work." I put the wine glass on the table, not realizing I drank half of it already.

"Yeah I would like that, is this the stuff you sell?" She picks up the basket, inspecting the contents.

Did she just sniff it? "Uh, yeah, I make all the products that are sold in the shop."

"Why don't you come to the club this weekend, Jasmine is going to be preforming." Sam snorts out a laugh, falling back on the couch holding her belly.

I feel the flames of embarrassment inching up my face. I punch Sam in the arm, but it just makes her laugh harder.

"Oh, what kind of performance?" Allya raises an eyebrow, smirking.

"Jasmine and her Dom are doing a live show center stage this weekend. Her very first." Sam sits up trying to reign in her laughter.

"Damn it, Sam." I throw a pillow at her, causing her to break out into a fit of giggles again.

Allya is trying desperately not to laugh, covering her mouth, and refusing to look at us. She picks up her wine glass, downing the red liquid. She covers her mouth again and I hear her snort. She is laughing.

"I would love to see that," she attempts to speak with a straight face.

"I'm so glad you guys are enjoying my pain here." I place my hand on my forehead, pretending to faint. Throwing them into another fit of giggles.

"Hey, I have an idea. We should do a girls night spa

kind of thing before Jasmine's performance. You know the whole mani, pedi, facial thing." Sam pulls me to sitting upright. Pure excitement etched on her face.

Allya looks just as excited. "Oh, Sam that sounds like so much fun. I haven't had girlfriends in forever."

We sat and chatted the rest of the night, making plans for the spa day. Sam's going to make sure Allya can get into the club for the weekend and Allya's going to come to the store sometime to start working.

Sam called the limo driver. We said our goodbyes as he pulled up out front. I like Allya, we all seemed to get along really well. It's nice to have some female companionship for once, that doesn't feel like some sort of competition.

The driver drops Sam and I at the club. I head up to bed while she goes down to find Marcus and Thomas to let them know we are back.

I stumble my way into the bedroom. I'm exhausted again, these all nighters are messing with my internal clock. I slip into the bed, wrapped in softness and the scent of Marcus. I sigh to myself, content, for once in my life, slipping into a dreamless sleep.

Chapter 14

Sam strolls through the club door, smiling like a kid in a candy store. I've not seen her like that in a hundred years Thomas raises an eyebrow at me in question. I just shrug my shoulders.

"Marcus, we need to talk." Sam jumps up on the bar stool beside me. "Thomas, can I get a shot of whiskey?"

"What's up Sam?" I turn to face her.

"Jasmine and I went to Allya's tonight, we stopped at the shop first. There were flowers for her again."

"Shit, Sam we got to figure out who is doing this. You have any ideas?"

"Not really, the flowers have such a strong smell, I couldn't scent anything else."

"All right, we'll figure out how to deal with that. What did you find out about Allya?" I drink the beer Thomas left on the bar for me.

"Well she's a shifter, I pulled her aside to let her know Jasmine doesn't know about the supernatural yet. So she didn't spill the beans, but she didn't really give a lot of background info on herself." Sam downs her shot, and shivers.

"What did you women decide then?"

"Well Jasmine offered her a job at the shop and I suggested a spa day before the big performance his weekend. Allya's all in for it."

"Wait, you invited Allya to the club?" I put the beer

back on the bar and just stare at her.

"Yeah, why?"

"Because she is Anthony's mate. Do you think he is going to be able to control himself? You know how long he's been looking."

Shock crosses her face. "Marcus I didn't think about that. Its just Jas and I hit it off so well with her, we wanted her to check out the club."

"I'll warn Anthony about it. By the way did you know Mia is still missing?"

"No, none of Anthony's shifters have been able to get a lead on her?"

"No, she just disappeared, no trail at all." I down the rest of my beer, handing the empty bottle to Thomas.

"I'll go out tomorrow night and see what I can dredge up. Thomas do you know where she liked to hunt at?" Sam turns to him.

"Yeah, she liked to go down by the docks, she always like being close to the water." Thomas stops cleaning the bar top and looks to Sam.

"Okay Thomas, I'll start down there tomorrow night." Sam hops off the bar stool and walks away.

I turn to Thomas, the pain etched on his face evident. Mia was his best friend, she knew all his secrets and now she was missing. I fear the hunters may have caught her. If she isn't already dead, death will be the best thing for her. Not many of us, vampire or shifter, can survive psychologically at the hands of the hunters. Yeah we are stronger and faster, but if caught, they starve us. Once weakened they experiment to find swifter faster ways to damage us, hunting for the perfect weapon. They strip us of our humanity, bringing the beast to the surface. The use all the things they know about us, the sensitivity to silver to damage our flesh. The hunters destroy our bodies, feeding us enough rotten animal blood to heal, so they can do it again. They have been known to keep one of us captive for months before finally allowing us to die.

"Thomas, you know if we find her, she may not be the same?"

"I know Marcus, if she can't be saved, I want to be the one to put her down."

"Are you sure about that?"

"Marcus it's the least I can do for her, to put her beast to rest, she wouldn't want to be a monster without humanity."

"That's your choice, I will make sure anyone that finds her knows to bring her in alive. We will try to save her first." I pat him on the shoulder and turn to head upstairs.

My love is asleep in my bed, how would I feel if she were taken, missing like Mia. I would tear the world apart till I found her that's how. She is my everything, my soul mate, my other half.

Her auburn hair fans out around her on the pillow. She looks like an angel, so perfect. A small smile plays across her lips. I slide into the bed beside her, she purrs and curls up against me, molding her body to mine. I wrap my arms around her, holding her tight as the rising sun pulls me into sleep.

Chapter 15

It's Friday night. Sam sent the drive to get Allya at her house. We are having a spa day in Marcus's condo. It's amusing to see a grown man flee in the face of woman with hot wax and nail polish. The beauticians brought all sorts of equipment with them to set up. Sam broke out some of Marcus's best wine.

Sam's cell rings. She answers and turns to me. "The driver is out back with Allya, I'm going to go down and bring her up."

"Okay, I'm going to crack open the wine."

I hear Sam and Allya giggling their way up the stairs. They stumble through the doorway. Allya is wearing a black leather pencil skirt and a green corset. She looks stunning.

"So you like the outfit I picked out?" Allya twirls in a circle.

" You look amazing, you'll fit right in."

We all head into the living room, carrying our wine glasses with us. Taking different seats around the space so the beauty team can get to work. The beauticians hand us robes, instructing us to strip and come back with those on.

A couple hours later we are all thoroughly waxed and painted. Sam and Allya opted for messy French braids with flowers strategically placed in a line down their backs. I chose loose waves, so my hair hangs free down my back. Sam and Allya head down to the club to get seats up front for support.

"Jasmine, I'm going to send Marcus up to get you, get your outfit on." Sam drags Allya out the door.

I'm wearing the new outfit I bought for Marcus and I'm freshly groomed, just like he likes. I'm wearing the cuffs he used the last time we went to the club. The elevator door dings and he steps into the room. .

My nerves are wound. I don't want to let him down tonight. I'm actually proud that he thinks I've come far enough to show off. He pulls me into his arms, smiling down. He slants his mouth over mine and I melt into his body. He runs his hands down my arms, leaving a trail of goose bumps in their wake. He takes a step back from me, spinning me around to take in all that I'm wearing. His breath hisses out through is lips. I swear his eyes flash that ominous glowing yellow as he takes in my new outfit. I'm wearing a blood red lace corset with sheer black stockings, no panties. The six-inch platform black strappy shoes make my legs look killer.

"Well isn't this a lovely outfit." Marcus pats my bare ass, sounding genuinely surprised with my choice of attire tonight, making me all bubbly inside to know I've pleased him.

"Come." He beckons me. I'm tingling everywhere he touches me. I have goose bumps raised onto my skin stifling a shiver while squeezes my ass cheek.

"There are a few more things we have to do to prepare you for tonight before we head to the club." Leading me to the sofa he guides me to a bending position with my ass high in the air and my shoulders on the cushions. I know where this is leading. He rubs the cool lube around my anus, pushing his finger in. I squirm at the sensation; he smacks my ass reminding me to be still. He puts in a second finger scissoring them around until my muscles start to relax. The broad head of the plug pushes into me. I'm instantly taking right to the edge of orgasm. He knows how much I like what he does to me. I never knew I would take to anal play so quickly, by the time he has the plug fully seated I'm panting for air. He helps me to a standing position and holds me until I regain some of my composure.

"I think a little more jewelry tonight will be appropriate for a public showing." His smile is wicked as he heads to the bedroom.

I wonder what else he has in mind, I dare not speak. He didn't ask a question merely stated what he wishes to do. He returns with a gold chain with some kind of device attached to it and a small velvet box. It looks like jewelry, but it's too long for a necklace. The box is beautiful, rich blue velvet. Marcus kneels in front of me placing the chain around my waist. I watch, intrigued by him giving me a necklace for my belly. As he fastens it around me I notice more chain attached to a gold sliding clip. He leans forward and runs his tongue along my slit. My clit instantly hardens, peeking out of its protective hood begging for attention. He slips the clip over it and tightens it down. It pinches, I gasp. He loosens it a little, but leaving enough pressure that my clit is exposed and open for his touch at any time. He makes me walk around the living room. The chain tugs on my clit every time I take a step, with the plug in my ass and this chain on my clit, I'm barely in control and we haven't went into the club yet. My breathing is ragged; I'm losing my composure.

"No coming yet." He tilts my chin to look in his eyes. . "Just breathe through it. It will make tonight that much more. Now for the final adornment." He opens the velvet box, inside is a beautiful thick gold omega chain with an M initial hanging on the front, a padlock on the back. He produces a key from his pocket. "I want you to wear my collar."

I know what this means, he is claiming me as his submissive. It is a form of ownership. Showing all who see it who I belong to, who I chose to be with, it is a commitment from him to me and I to him.

"Yes Sir." I finally breathe the words out of my mouth past the lump that has formed in my throat. He wants to keep me. He wants everyone to know I'm his and not just for the scene tonight, for always.

He slips the heavy gold necklace around my neck, when the padlock clicks into place I immediately relax. I'm truly his.

"Let's go luv. We've a long night ahead of us." He ushers me to the elevator and down into the basement of the club.

Chapter 16

She looks amazing tonight. I can't believe she chose a blood red outfit. How fitting for this evening, her arousal wafts around me like a beacon. Her juices flowing onto her thighs as she walks, her body trembling on the verge of orgasm. All eyes are on her, as I lead her through the club, they know she's mine. They are excited about seeing her submit to me. I lead her to one of the tables in the corner of the largest playroom of the dungeon area. I'm going to let her watch a few scenes herself before we do our own. Sam and Allya bring drinks over and sit with us.

"You look a little pale Jas, you okay?" Sam reaches across and takes her hand.

Jasmine turns her head to me and I nod. "You can speak freely with Sam and Allya luv."

"God, Sam I'm so nervous." Jasmine fingers the collar around her neck.

"You'll do fine, I swear." Sam smiles.

Jasmine's body relaxes as she leans into me.

"Okay girls." I look to Sam and Allya. "Better go get your seats."

I turn to Jasmine. "It's almost time for your performance are you ready?" I smell her arousal spike in response. Tonight is the night everything I taught her, we show to the public.

"I'm nervous and excited." She turns and wraps her arms around my neck.

I'm pleased with her progress in communication. She's made great strides in expressing herself, her wants, and needs.

"Good, the stage is being prepared for us, it's our turn." I smile

This is her first time in the lower level of the club; everyone down here is something other than human. I'm hoping after tonight she will piece together the question flitting through her mind about things she has seen and ask them.

Sam and Allya have taken up seats in the front row. I'm glad Jasmine has found friends in my circle that she gets along with so well. It'll make her transition easier. The stalker she has will have to be dealt with at some point, but at least I know she will be protected at the club.

The scenes we walk by on the way to the stage are more extreme than upstairs. The welts and marks on the subs much harsher than she has been exposed too. The smell of blood and sex is heavy in this area. Her body tensing as we get closer to the stage. I release the leash on the cuff, taking her hand in mine.

"It'll be okay." I turn taking her in my arms.

"I'm nervous." Her body trembles with fear.

"I'd never hurt you luv, you know that right?"

"I'm not afraid of you. What if I embarrass you?" she whispers into my chest.

"Do you trust me?" I stroke my hand down the soft waves of her hair.

"Yes." She looks up at me with love in her eyes.

"Okay then, lets get started, you will enjoy yourself. I'll make sure of it." I lead her to the edge of the stage.

Chapter 17

We arrive at the stage. It's a large raised circle in the middle of the room. There are chairs all the way around it. So observers can see from all sides. This is it. I'm getting up there and he is going to bare my soul to all these onlookers. I'm lucky to be here. Marcus is dropped dead gorgeous and he wants to show me off. With one last cleansing deep breath, I follow Marcus up the steps and allow him to shackle me to the hook hanging overhead. My toes barely reach the ground this position thrusts my breast forward. It pulls on the chain he has around my waist and tugs on my clit. I gasp. I'm so turned on, that little tug has me racing towards orgasm. God, we haven't even started yet.

There are so many people down here ready to watch us. The thought that all these people want to see me makes me feel sexy and powerful. Marcus walks around me building the tension. He strokes my arms, with the slightest touch, raising goose bumps on my skin. The anticipation stealing my breath. He removes the ties from my corset peeling it from my body. My body trembles with desire.

Naked, except for the chain around my waist, I am on display for the whole room. There's a whoosh of air as he brings the flogger close to my skin. He's ready to start. The first contact is more of a caress, readying me for the others. Each strike becoming quicker, harder until he covers my entire back. My skin is warm, the heat spreads through my body, coursing tingles across my skin. He moves into my line of site, twirling the flogger in circles. The first strike across my breast seizes the air in my lungs. My nipples already tight hard buds, each swat of the flogger. By the time Marcus finishes his rounds with the flogger my body is beaded with sweat. I'm a mass of desire begging for permission to cum.

"Please, Marcus. I need." My body sways towards him, unable to finish the sentence.

I'm so close. I need him to touch me one more time and I'll explode. He knows it too because, the flogging ends. I swear his eyes are glowing yellow as he smiles that sadistic knowing smile. Removing my shackles from the chain he leads me to the bed at the edge of the stage. He lays me down in the center and spreads out my arms and legs, hooking my cuffs to the rings on the posts of the bed. Helpless, bound spread eagle, only able to beg him to finish me. I need to come so bad my breath coming in ragged short gasps.

"Deep breaths my love, it's not time yet." He kisses my temple, pushing the sweat-streaked hair from my face. "I am going to remove the clit clamp now."

Marcus removes the chain from my waist. He slides the clamp from my clit, it throbs as the blood flows back into it. It feels swollen, like it's three times its normal size. It's peeking out of its hood, begging for attention. He positions himself between my spread legs and runs his hands over my nipples stopping to flick and pinch them. I can see the bulge in his pants. It looks as if his leathers are going to burst. The muscles in his chest ripple as he moves his arms over my body. Working his way down to my stomach and inching towards my waiting pussy.

"Please." I moan no longer able to hold it in. I thrust my hips as far as I can reach, seeking contact with something, anything that would take away the ache in my body. He runs his finger over my outer lips bringing his glistening finger to his mouth. I see fangs as he inserts his finger into his mouth and sucks my juices from the digit. I can't think straight, I am so turned on my brain is misfiring. I'm seeing things. He leans down running his tongue up my slit. It is almost more sensation than I can take. I don't know if I can hold out any longer.

"Sir, please I can't." I pant and gasp the sentence from my mouth. My throat is dry, my body is shaking, needing release.

He reaches down freeing his raging hard on from his leather's. It curves towards his belly, precum glistening on the tip. I lick my lips in anticipation. He smiles knowing full well what I'm thinking then. He runs his hands over my thighs and down the crease of my leg. He is so close to my pussy the heat from his body radiates into me. He trails his fingers down farther tapping the plug I'm wearing, my ass clenches with delight.

"I'm going to take this out now, because tonight you will no longer be an anal virgin." Marcus taps the plug again, sending ripples of sensation through me.

A look of shock must cross my face because he leans over me and quietly for only my ears. "Relax, I'll never hurt you. Trust me."

I nod in acknowledgment and he removes the plug. My anal muscles clench looking for something to grab onto. The empty feeling strange, after being stuffed full all night. That plug isn't nearly the size of his penis. I'm still a little nervous, but I trust him.

I chance a look around the room, positive these people's eyes are glowing. It's like looking out over a field at night, seeing the fireflies glowing in the darkness. It must be a trick of the lights human eyes don't glow.

***

God, she looks amazing all bound up for my pleasure. The candle light flickers off her skin, making her look like a bronze statue shining in the sun. She's trembling with need now. This is right where I want her to be to take her anally. I want her unrestrained and on edge. I want to fuck that sweet mouth of hers first.

I slither up her body, straddling her chest. Jasmine obediently opens her mouth as my cock touches her pretty red lips. Her mouth a warm wet haven. She sucks and swirls her tongue around the ridge of my cock. It's like coming home. I wrap my fingers in her hair, pushing my cock hard into her mouth, until it hits the back of her throat. Jasmine gags, tears, glisten in her eyes. I pull back and ram my cock in hard again. . She looks so beautiful with her mascara staining her cheeks, her unshed tears shimmering in the light. I thrust in a couple more times, the last time holding myself in the back of her throat. I know she can't breathe, but her body remains relaxed, no alarm crosses that beautiful face. Her complete and total submission is mine. She'll let me do anything trusting I know what is best. I don't want to cum in her sweet mouth, not tonight. I slide slowly down her body. Stopping to suck and bite a nipple. She arches to meet me, thrusting her breast farther into my mouth, gladly biting her nipple harder, drawing a husky moan from her lips. Jasmine writhes on he bed, pushing her hips into the air seeking contact with anything. I glide the rest of the way down her body, pulling her clit into my mouth. Her breath hisses through clenched teeth as her body stiffens.

"Not yet my sweet" I move from her clit leaning back on my knees, rubbing the head of my cock over the swollen bundle of nerves, coating myself in her wetness.

Her breath is coming faster, more ragged with each pass across her clit. I reach down and unhook her leg cuffs, lifting her hips, bringing her ass to the head of my cock. I need to see her face as I breech her untried hole. I push against her, feeling the moment I pass the tight outer ring of muscles. Jasmine pushes against me, driving my cock deeper into her in the most forbidden of holes. Her body is hot, branding me like rays of the sun, her muscles ripple along my shaft. I enter her slowly inch by agonizing inch. It's a tight fit even with the stretching she did this week. Finally, buried to the hilt, holding her still, letting her body adjust to the invasions The whimpers escaping form her mouth are driving me crazy.

"Please, Sir, please, Fuck me now." She tries to thrust herself onto me, begging.

Not waiting another second I pull out and plunge back in. She grips my cock, sucking on it with her muscles. Her body pulls taut as a bowstring, the orgasm imminent. I pull her hips into me with each thrust, pumping faster and harder into her body.

"Sir, please may I come now? Please Marcus. I can't." Jasmine's head thrashes on the bed, tears leaking from her eyes.

I thrust my cock deep in her ass, reaching down to pinch her clit. "Now my love, come for me."

Her body convulses around me. I feel each pulse and throb on my cock. It pulls my orgasm from my body. I let loose a primal scream my fangs fully extended. I see the others in the room. Their eyes are all aglow now too. The moment recognition sets in I have fangs. Jasmine screams. A blood-curdling wail that chills me to my soul. She passes out cold. I unchain her picking her up in my arms. Thomas grabs a bottle of wine and a bag of blood, following me to the elevator. Sam and Allya appear at my side, pity etched on both of their faces. I hadn't meant to let her see me lose complete control of the beast.

"Is there anything we can do Marcus?" Sam strokes

Jasmines sweat matted hair.

"I was hoping that after tonight, seeing the flashes of fangs, she might ask the questions floating around in her mind. I didn't wish to frighten her so badly." I turn from them and head into the elevator.

"If you need us, you know how to reach me. We are here for you or her." Sam takes Allya' arm and walks away.

Chapter 18

I awake alone, in the darkness. Looking around I realize I'm in Marcus's bed. I remember the fangs, the glowing eyes. The whole room's eyes were glowing. Grabbing my neck I quickly check for marks.

"No one bit you." Marcus's voice floats towards me from the corner of the room.

"What are you? What did you do to me? Why didn't you tell me? Are you all like that?" I'm pretty sure I am rambling. I don't care. I'm more scared now than I've ever been in my life. Am I just some sacrifice? Is he going to have me for dinner now? "How long have I been out?"

"Calm down Jasmine. I'm a vampire. I'm sure you figured that out. I didn't tell you for this reason here. I wanted you to know me for who I am as a person before you judge me as an animal. You have been out for about an hour." He answers every question I asked never leaving the shadows of the corner of the room.

"How am I supposed to calm down? That whole room was full of your kind. How am I supposed to believe you aren't going to eat me or someone else down there will?"

I'm close to hysterics. I'm in a building full of God knows what. My heart seizes in my chest, I love him, or thought I did.

"Jasmine, please listen to me. I'll tell you whatever you want to know, I need you to try to remember the trust you had for me before you knew what I am. I've never hurt you. Can we please just talk about this?"

Marcus actually sounds sad. I still can't see him. He hasn't made a move to get close to me and he is right I had trusted him and he never hurt me.

"Okay," I sigh, "I'll hear you out, but you need to come into the light where I can see you. I'm not going to talk to a shadow."

I hear the rustle of clothes as he stands from the chair to come closer to the bed. I suddenly feel more vulnerable than anytime we played together. I'm still naked in his bed alone and he isn't human.

"I'm not going to hurt you." He reaches the edge of the bed and sits down making no move to touch me. "I'll tell you anything you want to know. All you have to do is ask the questions, I 'll not lie about anything.

"What are your plans for me? How old are you? I know you eat real food, do you drink blood too? Does the sunlight really pose a threat to you? Why aren't you cold to the touch? Why does your heart still beat? Why me?" I curl the pillow against my chest, I know I'm rambling. I want to get all my questions out before I change my mind and before he changes his.

"Well, let's start with I am 200 years old."

My mouth gapes in shock. I hadn't guessed him over 29.

"Yes, I eat real food. I do need blood to survive. My heart still beats, I can control how fast or slow it does. I can make it like a normal human or slow it down to conserve energy. The blood that I consume flows through my veins just like your blood does and that is what keeps me from feeling cold. If I haven't fed for a long time I need to keep my heart rate slower to conserve energy until I can feed again and I'll feel cooler to the touch."

I must be staring at him because he stops talking then. He still hasn't answered my question about what his plans are for me, I have other questions that need answered too.

"Do you have any supernatural powers like in the books? Super strength, super speed, flying, mind control?"

These were the things I really need to know. Did he control my mind, to make me want these things or are these really my own feelings for him. This would be the deciding factor or whether or not he can be trusted.

"I'm stronger than a human. I can move fast enough to be blurred by human eyes. Yes, vampires can fly. I can jump very high also, but don't control minds. I can read some human minds and manipulate memories if needed."

I'm strangely relieved by his answers. Happy that my feelings are my own. I don't sense any lies from him. His body posture remains relaxed, but guarded like he is ready for me to scream or attack him. He hasn't ever hurt me though and aside from scaring the shit out of me, has done nothing to warrant me not trusting him.

"Can I see your fangs?"

I must have taken him by surprise by the look of shock that crosses his face before he quickly shunts it away. Hell it surprises me too.

"Yes"

That is all he says, making no move to get closer to me. He simply turns his head towards me and opens his mouth. Forgetting about my nakedness, I move onto my knees to get close enough to inspect them. They are gleaming white and look sharp.

"Can I touch them?"

I can't help myself I need to feel them, touch them. They are actually beautiful. He just nods. His body is still as a statue as I run my fingers over his mouth and across his fangs. They are so smooth, so hard, and the ends so sharp. They are really scary when you aren't expecting it, but I feel my pussy clench with need being this close to him again. Suddenly he jerks away from me.

"Jasmine, I can't be this close to you when you are naked and aroused. I smell your arousal, another trait I have is a very sensitive nose. I want you too badly. I'm barely in control now and your arousal is pushing me to the edge."

My cheeks heat, my face flames with embarrassment. I didn't know he smells my arousal, but that would explain why he always knows just what I need. The fact he can read my mind probably isn't helping either.

"I'm sorry, I didn't mean to make you uncomfortable. Your fangs are wondrous." I sit back on the bed, hugging his pillow "You never answered me on what your plans are for me?"

"I would like to offer to turn you into a vampire. I

want to be with you forever Jasmine. I love you. You are my soul mate. I have searched the world for you for two hundred years, ever since my turning. I knew the moment I laid eyes on you. That you were the only one who would make my eternal existence mean anything."

I am taken aback by the depth of emotion in his voice. I need time and space to think about this. I have responsibilities in the world. I don't have any family left that would notice a change in habits for me, but I still need time to think.

"How long will you give me to decide and if I decide not too what happens then?"

I need to know what my options are. I don't want to end up on the menu if I say no.

"I'll give you until the next full moon to decide. If you chose that this is not a life you think you can live or you don't want to spend eternity with me. The events at the club, your time with me and Sam will be altered in your mind as if it never happened."

It's a blunt answer, but nothing I didn't expect. How can he let me know about his existence if I chose not to be with him? It would make it unsafe.

"Okay. Then I would like to get dressed and go home so I can think about this. I'll have an answer for you before the next full moon. I promise. This is a lot for me to consider. I will not make this decision lightly."

I owe him at least some thought on this. I don't know if I can do it, but if I can, for anyone it is Marcus. The next full moon is only seven days away.

"I'll get the car to take you home. Your clothes are in

the bathroom if you would like to clean up before you leave." He makes to stand from the bed. I stay him with a hand on his arm.

"Marcus?" I lean over and brush my lips across his in a whisper of a kiss. "I'll see you soon." I get up and head to the bathroom leaving him sitting on the bed.

Chapter 19

I'm home now and more than slightly confused it is about three in the morning. I'm sure sleep is not on the agenda tonight. So setting up the Internet, I go about finding anything I can, related to vampires or soul mates. There is a plethora of information out there most of it sounds crazy and I'm positive none of it's actual first hand knowledge.

There is one site telling me how dangerous and bloodthirsty a vampire is. There's a contact number that is local to the area. They seem to have the most accurate information on abilities and weaknesses. I'll have to ask Marcus if he has an affinity to silver. It seems these people on this site think so. I'm assuming these are the type of people that are the reason behind the mind altering should I choose not to turn. I wonder how much more these people know than me.

The sun is rising as I walk onto the balcony of my room to watch. The way the sky turns from inky blue to pink, then the shimmering blue of the summer sky. I've always loved the feel of the sun on my skin, the way it manages to relax and warm my soul. I still don't know what to do. I love Marcus, he makes me feel special, loved. I'm not sure I'm ready to give up my mortal life. I love my little shop and making my poultices and creams, my little garden where I grow all my own herbs and flowers. Sure I could still run an Internet business, but would really like to be able to continue having my own store. I guess this is the kind of things I need to talk to him about. I don't know if I can drink blood, the thought of the metallic tang of iron and copper coating my throat is enough to gag me.

Finally at nine in the morning exhaustion over takes me, I slide stiffly into the sheets of my bed. Sleep is quick to take me under and I dream:

It's the cool of night and the moon is high in the sky. The trees are inky blobs against the night sky; the clearing is lit up by the full moon. It is just Marcus standing out there I see him all alone in the center. He appears to be praying to some God. I inch out of the clearing towards him. He turns to me eyes blazing like the fires of hell, his fangs flashing white in the darkness. He is naked from the waist up his chest is glistening in the moonlight. I watch as a woman who looks like me approaches him no words are said. As she sits next to him in the rock circle and lays her head on his shoulder. He welcomes her into his arms and holds her tight. I feel his love for her. I watch, as she shakes her head no. She has decided. She will not be with him not as a vampire. I feel the sadness of his soul wash over me, the pain nearly crushing my heart. The scene changes, I see Marcus again; he is holding a dying woman's hand as she lay in her bed. Her breathing is faint, her lungs rattle with every inhalation. She coughs and sputters. The woman opens her eyes and I see myself in her. She draws his hand to her lips and kisses it. She takes her last breath. The scream that he makes will rival the wail of a banshee. The pain of her loss, the pain he feels, breaks my heart. How many times has he found me and I denied him? How much torture can one soul bare? I couldn't go on without him, yet I've made him continue on without me for over a hundred years. I've tortured his soul and lived my lives allowing him to find me and love me only to deny his gift and leave him again. He is like coming home, warm, safe, and comforting. I need to be held by him in his solid embrace for all eternity.

I awake with a start, completely aware of my dream. Tears streaming down my face, the ache in my chest and deeper in my soul crushing the life from me. I need him. I cannot fathom living without knowing him or not being with him. I look at the alarm clock on the stand. It's four in the afternoon. I jump out of bed and shower quickly. I dress in black skinny jeans and a red spaghetti strap tank top, leaving my hair down. I grab my stilettos and run to the phone. I call the number for the driver. He can be here to get me in fifteen minutes. The sun hasn't set yet, but it is getting low in the sky.

The limo pulls up out front, I sprint down my steps and slide into the back seat before the driver even has a chance to get out. Lost in my own thoughts. I don't realize how long we've been in the car until the door opens. I step out of the vehicles, face to face with a strange driver and in the middle of nowhere. Panic sets in, I punch at him, kicking him in the shins. He backhands me and the world goes black.

Muffled voices, drag me out of my unconscious state.

I refuse to open my eyes, trying to figure out what the hell is going on. Oh my God, its the serial killer or the stalker that's been after me. Shit. I try to focus on the voices; I can't make out any words. Thump, thump, thump. Hard boot steps echo towards me. The smell of mud and blood swirl through the air. A hand brushes the hair from my face. I try not to cringe, feigning sleep instead. I figure the longer I'm out the less than can hurt me right?

"What the hell did you hit her for?"

That voice sounds oddly familiar. I keep my eyes shut, hoping they will give away some detail to where we are.

"Damn it James, you didn't tell me the bitch was crazy."

James, that son of a bitch, he's behind this? No longer scared, I open my eyes, taking a swing at James sitting on the edge of the couch with me.

"You bastard, you kidnapped me?"

"Calm down Jas, it's not what you think." He grabs my arms pinning them to my sides, crushing my body against his, as he stands.

"Put me the fuck down asshole." I kick my feet, landing my heels into his shins.

"I'll put you down, when you calm down and listen to me." He squeezes me tighter, forcing the air from my lungs.

"Fine, talk."

James lets go of me and I plop down on the couch. He turns to look at me, giving me his fake charming smile. I want to gag, his dirty blonde hair, slicked back like some fifties punk. His watered down blue eyes, pale in comparison to anything I've seen lately.

"I'm just trying to help you, Jas." He reaches for my leg.

"I scoot out of reach, rubbing the sore spot on my cheek. "Yeah that's why your buddy here slugged me."

James face flames red with anger, he's so easy to bait. His buddy has the nerve to look embarrassed.

"Ron wasn't supposed to hurt you Jas, I just want to help you." He scoots closer on the couch, pinning me to the armrest.

His vile breath washes over me, coursing a shiver of disgust through my body. James apparently takes it as a good sign and curls his arm over my shoulder.

"What gives you the impression I need help?" I put my hand on his chest pushing him away from me.

"Jasmine, do you know what kind of things frequent that club you been going to?"

I decide playing dumb is safest at this point until I figure out exactly what he is talking about. How could lazy ass James, know anything about that club.

"I know what they do in the club, I have no idea what kind of things you are talking about."

" I know your going to think I'm crazy, but those things there aren't human. They are vampires and shifters?" He puts his arm around my shoulder, pulling me against his chest.

"James you are crazy, vampires and shifters? Seriously, are you watching to many horror movies?"

"Let's get you something to eat and cleaned up, then we can talk about it more." He stands up, pulling me up with him and twining our fingers together.

I resist the urge to jerk my hand from his, deciding it's best to play along until I figure out where the hell we are and just how many people are here. He leads me out of the living room into a large country kitchen. The appliances are old, and yellowing from age. The water faucet runs a dirty brown before clearing, as he turns the sink on. He fills a glass with water and hands it to me. I drink it, so I don't have to talk to him any more. I look out the window over the sink there are trees as far as I can see. We are apparently in the middle of the woods somewhere.

The stomping of boots draws my attention to the back door. Three more men walk in. I swear I just got swallowed by some cheap B movie. Flannel shirts, muddy jeans, and facial hair. Good God.

"This is Larry." James points to mister red beard.

"Joe." James motions to the scrawny guy in the middle. "And this here is Martin."

They all nod and continue to trek stink and mud through the kitchen, leaving grubby fingerprints on everything they touch.

"James, you kidnap me, then tell me tales of non human creature, and now you want me to have dinner with all your goonies?" I stalk towards the back door. "You are crazy."

James grabs me from behind, pulling me away from the door. "Where do you think your going? It's dark and none of us are driving you to town. You don't even know where you are."

"What the hell do you want?" I wiggle out of his grip, turning to glare at him.

"You are going to eat and then I'll show you just what I'm talking about." He leads me to the kitchen table, forcing me to sit in the chair.

Dinner consists of canned soup and cold sandwiches, in the company of redneck central. The slobs slop more food on the table and the front of their shirts than they eat. I swirl the murky soup around in the bowl, not really hungry. I just want to get this night over with. I don't know what James is so sure he knows, but I can't imagine this gang is all that organized.

After the sun goes down Larry, Joe, Martin and Ron leave us alone. James clears the table and through the bowls in the sink. He turns towards me, leveling his gaze on me.

"Are you ready to see, what you are hanging out with?"

"James enough with the dramatics already. I want to see what you think I need to and go home." I stand and head to the back door, turning to wait for him to show me what he knows.

"All right, but stay back and don't get to close." He takes my hand and leads me out the back door to a run down barn.

Chapter 20

"Marcus, Jasmine isn't at her house." Sam's voice rouses me out of my sulking.

"What do you mean she isn't at her house?"

"Well I went over to check on her and I can't get any answer at her door. There isn't any trace of a heartbeat in there either."

"Shit, Sam. Do you think she ran?" I stare out the window into the starless night. Jasmine wouldn't take off like that, or would she?

The elevator door dings open and Jake steps into the room. I turn to him, rage pouring off his body in waves.

"Jake what is it?"

"Marcus, we have a problem. The limo driver was found out in the alley unconscious tonight. The limo is still missing. It was the driver who was supposed to take Jasmine home."

Fear and rage vie for dominance in my soul. The suite takes on a red haze, as anger wins the battle. The sound in heightens as my beast takes full reign of my system.

I turn to Sam. Her eyes glow red with her own rage.

"Gather the others, we are going hunting for my bride." The sound of my voice echo's unnaturally as the beast speaks.

"Jake, gather the pack. Call Anthony, everyone is going on this hunt," Sam growls.

Jake exits the room, to gather the shifters. Sam heads

down to gather the remaining vampires in the club. Tonight we hunt for blood and love.

We look like an army heading to war. I guess we are, in a way. Thomas is here, if we find Mia. He is going to try to save her. I'm going to rip my way through bodies, not stopping until I find my love. I've waited to long for her to slip away now, by the hands of a hunter. Allya has come, to help. She has grown fond of Jasmine in the short time she has been here. The pack is ready we are starting the search at Jasmine's house.

I smell the lingering scent of a man outside her windows. Someone has been here watching her.

"Sam, someone has been in the bushes. I am going around back. Get the shifters over here to see if they can single out a fresh trail." Not waiting to see if Sam does what I ask, I head to the back. The flowers out here have been trampled down too. Someone has been here frequently.

"Marcus!" Sam yells around the house.

I swoop to her side. "What is it Sam?"

"There's a male scent mixed with Jasmine's down by the rode and fresh tracks from a car heading out of town. We aren't sure we can track the car once the scent mixes with the others on the road."

"Damn it Sam! We have to find her."

"If the same people that took her have Mia, we need to go back to the dock and see if we can pick up that trail."

That's what I love about Sam. Even in the middle of a

crisis her mind functions like a master hunter.

"Gather everyone up then, let's head to the docks."

Thomas picks up Mia's scent as soon as we get to the shore. "She was taken from here. The scent of her blood still stains the grounds." The pain of loss etched clearly in his eyes.

"Can you follow it?"

"I can Marcus, hopefully we are not too late." Thomas shifts into his wolf and sprints off into the direction of the woods.

The rest of us follow him quickly through the streets of town, nothing more than blurs to the humans mingling on the streets.

Thomas tracks as far as the edge of the woods near the back edge of the wolf retreat. A shiver races up my spine, this close to our haven. Anthony's eyes bore in to me, his anger palpable in the night air. This is his home, his land, and it has been infiltrated.

"I can't believe they have been under my fucking nose so long." Anthony stalks along the edge scenting the air.

"Anthony, I live on this land too and yet I had no idea either." I walk into the edge of the tree line, straining to hear any sounds not of the night. I don't understand how Mia's scent could just leave off at the edge of the woods. There isn't a road here that any of us know of.

"Thomas, are you sure you can't scent anything further?" The air around him cracks and pops. The human Thomas stands before me.

"It's strange she just disappears right here. Not even a

trace left."

"Can you smell any humans or anything out of the ordinary?" I scent the air and smell the faintest trace of diesel fuel.

"I smell fuel and oil." His eyes glint and he shifts to wolf, taking off into the woods.

"Anthony, it's time for the hunt." I take to the air sensing Sam beside me. The other vamps fall in line behind us.

On the ground below the shifters take to the woods. The call of their animals ringing throughout the silent night. The cool night air whispers in my ears, songs of lost souls. The hunt tonight, important to our entire community. Not only for the return of my love, but in the hopes that Mia can be saved or find peace. The scent of Jasmine rakes across my senses. My body tumbles out of the night sky.

"Marcus, what they hell?" Sam lands beside me, pulling me to my feet.

"Do you smell that? Jasmine is around here."

"I smell her, Marcus stay here wait for the shifters. We need a plan." Sam yanked my arm stopping me from heading in the direction of the scent.

"Damn it Sam."

"Damn it nothing. Marcus you will do this right. I know you love her, but no sense in getting us all killed."

Thomas breaks into the clearing first. His hackles raised, lips curled back in a snarl. The air sizzles, he walks over to me human once again.

"We need a plan?"

"So Sam tells me."

Anthony leads the rest of the shifters into the clearing. The crack and pop of the air, sounds like a firing squad, as everyone shifts back to human. We huddle around an area assigning signals and forest area to cover now that we have a fresh scent to follow. Anthony, Sam, Thomas and I team up to head to the West side. Michael, Allya, and Jake head for the North end. Jenny, a female wolf shifter, takes a group of shifters and young vamps back towards the South, to check for Mia's scent. Micah, the young vamp Sam had taken on in the club, take Steve and his friends to the Eastern quarter. With or without the girls we all agree to meet back at my house an hour before sunrise.

"Let's go people. I'm tired of waiting. I need to find her." I stalk off into the woods, Sam and Thomas right behind me.

The scent of stale blood and death assault my senses as we head deeper into the woods. The moon hides behind the clouds, afraid to look upon the death that will come tonight. The nocturnal animals have taken to hiding. The hunt is on, even the predators of nature hide in the wake of the supernatural beings.

The screams of torture rake across my skin, sending shivers in their wake. The wails of agony echo through the night, bouncing off the trees and reverberating into my soul. We stalk the edge of the clearing, spying the run down shack. The screams are coming from the barn out back. There are two distinct sounds of terror coming from the barn.

Jake and his group slip in behind us. " We will circle around the back. I will signal you when we are in position."

"We will wait for you, signal the others, I want no hunter left alive." I turn my back on him, concentrating on the piercing cries from the barn.

Chapter 21

The cloying scent of decay and stale blood wafts through the dusky dank air. James leads me into the barn, slivers of moonlight wink through the slatted roof. The rotted wood creaks and groans. The banshee wails and agonizing screams, slithers along my spine. My legs frozen in terror, shuffling along as James drags me in to see.

"Look at the monsters you hang around with at that club." James jerks my face to stare into the corner of the barn.

Chained to the wall, a petite form cowers in the corner. Her dress, filthy and ragged. The once white material now streaked with grime, her hair matted in tangles.

"James what they hell, you are torturing women in here?" I jerk from him, trying to get the women in the corner.

She levels glowing eyes on me, lit with the fires of hell. She snarls, revealing yellowed fangs, dripping with saliva. Her ashen skin peeling from her face, congealed blood dripping from her chin. The woman lunges at me, faster than I can register with my eyes. I fall banging my head into the hard floor of the barn. The stars swim in my vision. The sounds of hissing and screeching ringing in my ears. I shuffle backwards on my ass, towards the doorway. The petite frame in the corner, yanking against a silver collar around her neck. The smell of burning flesh bombards my senses, turning I heave, spewing forth the soup from dinner. My body wracked with tremors, the violent shudders seize my soul as the vile stench surrounds me.

"James what did you do?" I crawl towards he door.

"I didn't do this." He waves a hand at the creature in the corner. "It is a monster, I am only showing you what they hide from you."

He picks up a dead rat, flinging it at the woman in the corner. She snatches it out of the air, ripping chunks of flesh and hair out of it, sinking fangs into it consuming the dead flesh. Her growls of rage, elicit shivers in my bones. Her eyes bore into me, licking her lips. She sways back and forth, a mesmerizing cadence.

"Come here my little one." Her tongue darts out catching the dribble of old blood running across her lips. "You smell so sweet, your fear a tantalizing bouquet." Her voice a sweet melody, draws me towards her.

"Jasmine, what they hell." James jerks me back against him.

"What?" I turn to him.

"Why would you walk over there like that?"

"I wasn't, what are you talking about?"

"You were just staring at her, then you were walking towards her. Hell I yelled at you three times, but you wouldn't answer."

"She was talking to me, didn't you hear her?"

"She has never talked Jasmine. She is a monster. Watch." James walks towards the stall on the right. He returns with a handful of items I can't discern.

The hiss and growl from the woman in the corner draw my attention to her. No longer worrying about what James is doing, I study her. Her once long dark hair matted to her head, the scalp showing in places where it has been ripped out. Her body covered in open seeping sores. Her nails long and sharp like claws of a bear. She stares at James, pacing back and forth on the end of the chain.

James flicks his wrist, something glints in the peeking moonlight. The woman recoils, screeching and holding her shoulder. Blood oozes across the tainted shift, her eyes blaze red. The wail of despair breaks from her lips, raising the hairs on my neck.

"James stop! You're hurting her." I jerk the remaining sliver spikes from his hands.

"What is wrong with you? It is a fucking monster, it will devour you while you sleep. Yet you want to protect it." He strides towards me, pushing me into the wall. James grabs my arms, pinning me to the worn wood. " These are not humans. They have no feelings. These creatures are killing machines, we need to know their weaknesses."

"I still think it's cruel. You are torturing her." I jerk from his grasp, heading back to the edge of the chain length.

I kneel down, out of reach of the woman in the chains. She peers at me, her head turning from side to side in confusion.

"Do you have a name?"

She claws at the skin on her arms, leaving rakes of bloody welts. She yanks at her hair, pulling clumps of it from the roots. Her voice, shrill as she screams in frustration. She rakes her nails along her face, peeling the ashen skin away in slivers. I reach for her hand to stop her. She grabs me and pulls me into the circle. Her arms encircle my throat as my feet kick uselessly on the floor. She pulls me into the corner, her vile breath bathing across my cheek. The sticky drool of her saliva rolling down my neck and into my shirt. She licks at my neck, my pulse hammering in my head. My life flashes before my eyes, as stinging fangs plunge into my neck. The first pull of her mouth burns fire through my veins, my only thought, is death.

For a moment the screams that envelope my ears, I believe belong to me. My body is ripped from the grips of the woman and strong, warm arms surround me. My body relaxes into the safe feeling poured into it, a warm tongue trails over the burning pain in my neck. My eyes flutter open to stare into the whiskey glowing gaze of Marcus.

"Jasmine, are you okay?" He strokes a hand through my hair.

"I'm fine." I struggle from his grasp, backing into the corner away from him and the monster on the chain.

My eyes flit around the barn seeking a way out. A growl of rage bubbles out of Marcus's mouth as James throws a silver spike into his shoulder. I cower back, watching the ensuing battle unfold. Sam is dangling Larry by the neck, blood pouring from where his arm should have been. His eyes glazed over with shock, she sinks her fangs into his neck, as a scream gurgles from his throat. A wolf burst into the barn, running to the woman in the corner. It pulls her chains loose and drags her out of the barn. Marcus has James by the throat, the empty look in his eyes, stokes a shiver of fear up my spine. I turn and run out of the barn, leaving the monsters and the hunters behind. The echoing screams chase, me into he night. I run. The forest swallows me, refusing me safe passage. The branches reach for me tearing at my skin, raising welts of blood. The branches behind me snap and crack. Someone is coming, they aren't going to let me go. I've seen too much. Arms wrap around my waist, halting my escape. Screaming, I kick and jerk, trying to free my body.

"Jasmine." The arms around me loosen and Sam turns me to face her.

"S...Sam?" I back away from her. She looks just like the same I knew. No glowing eyes, no long sharp fangs, but I'm so confused.

I drop to my knees, sinking into the muddy dank ground. The tears pour freely from my eyes. The sobs wrack shudders in my body. My stomach turns as the vile memories of death and blood, swamp my senses. The visions invade my mind, and I lose my grip on reality. Screaming and sobbing, I pound my fists in the ground.

"I just want to go home." I look up at Sam, her own

eyes glisten with tears. She nods her head and picks me up. The last thing I see are the tops of the trees as we head over them, then my mind gives out and the world goes black.

Chapter 22

I wake up alone in my room. The sunlight filtering though the windows. The smell of rotten blood still clinging to my clothes.

"It wasn't a nightmare. Shit." I get out of bed and head to the shower.

The rust colored water swirls into the drain, washing away the scent of death. The dismay racking my heart isn't washed away as easily. I lean my forehead against the wall of the shower, letting the hot water stream over my body. My mind wanders though the jumble of memories from last night.

James is dead, I know with certainty. The vacant look in his eyes as I ran from the barn forever burned into my brain. My body shivers with thoughts of Marcus's fangs sunk deep into his neck, the gurgling sounds of James's life fading away.

My heart constricts with pain and loss. Not for James, but Marcus. The demanding lover, the patient teacher, the one my soul longs for. I can't fathom being without him and my chest aches with emptiness. Hot tears burn my face mixing with the steam from the shower. A sob breaks from my lips, at thoughts of life without Marcus. Can I trust him though? I don't know, my heart breaks for him, but my mind fears the monster within.

I step out of the shower, my limbs feeling as heavy as my heart. I shuffle downstairs, dragging my weary soul into the kitchen. This is what despair feels like. Death to the hope and love in the world.

"Fuck, I need to make a decision." I start the coffee maker and boot up the computer. It's going to be a long day.

I search vampire myths and lore, looking for anything that tells me they aren't monsters. I find the romanticized versions strewn all around. The only site taking about blood lust are hunter sites. This isn't helping. My heart still aches; a soul deep yearning to run to Marcus, but my mind revolts the idea of being dinner.

The memory of that woman sinking her fangs deep into my neck and pulling the life from me still burns deep. My hand goes to my neck seeking the wounds from the attack. I feel the smooth unmarred skin under my fingers.

"Marcus." Hot tears blur my vision of the screen.

He saved me, healed me, and I ran from him. My human brain, unable to understand my heart's call.

I slam my hands against the keyboard, spilling coffee all over the desk. "Damn it!"

I'm still afraid, still confused and this isn't helping. I've no one to talk to. What am I going to do? Can't very well call anyone to ask for help sorting through this.

My heart still races at the memories of the glowing eyes, tracking my movements in the barn. The yellowed saliva dripping fangs sends shivers up my spine. "Shit. I need to do something."

I head back into the kitchen taking the dried herbs down from the cupboard. The mundane task of mixing lotions and poultices eases my mind. The aroma of the herbs soothes my soul. I breathe the calming scents of lavender and chamomile as I stir the herbs into the creamy lotion base.

The sun is setting low in the sky when I emerge from my meditative mixing. The sky streaked in pinks and purples. I head into the living room, opting for a cup of hot tea, instead of coffee. I haven't made any decisions yet, but at least I am not in a panicked state of mind now.

I sink into the couch, letting the smooth velvet fabric wrap around my body. It's a comforting embrace, a normalcy I've missed today.

The soft wrap of knuckles on my front door causes me to spill the hot tea down the front of my robe.

"Damn it." I get up, checking the peephole on the door.

It's Sam and Allya. I don't know if I can deal with this tonight.

"What do you guys want?"

"Jas, we just want to talk." Sam peers through the peephole back at me.

I open the door and wave them in. " I don't know what you think you can tell me, but come on in."

I sit on the chair opposite the couch, making Allya and Sam sit together away from me. My skin breaks out in a clammy sweat and my heart races. Fear racks my system as flashes of Sam's glowing eyes and fangs invade my mind.

"So what do you want to talk about?" I wipe my sweaty palms on my robe; I didn't even bother getting dressed today.

"Jasmine, we aren't going to hurt you. We are still your friends." Sam leans forward resting her elbows on her knees.

"Well, then why are you here? I mean do you have anything to add to the horror I witnessed last night. Fuck, Sam your eyes were glowing and you killed a man. Allya, is there something you need to tell me about you?" I jump out of the chair pacing around the room. My arms are waving as anger floods my system.

These people, or whatever they are lied to me. They used me. They played with my heart and made me a fool.

"Jas, calm down." Allya stands up heading towards me.

"Oh no, you don't." I hold my hands up, warding off her approach. "Talk, but stay on the couch or get out."

"Fine. I'm a shifter." She plops heavily on the couch, crossing her arms over her chest. "You happy now."

The look of hurt on her face, almost undoes me, but not quite. I'm the only human in the room and they knew it.

"So nice of you to tell me now." I sit in the chair, rubbing my burning eyes.

"Jasmine, will you let me give our side of the story? At least give me that, I've never hurt you." Sam levels her gaze on me; the pain etched on her beautiful face breaks my resolve.

"Fine, I will listen, but I'm not making any promises about coming back to that club or anything right now."

"That's fair enough." Sam brushes her pale locks from her face, staring at the wall. "Let me start by telling you that, the woman that was in there was named Mia. She was taken from the docks two weeks ago."

"James had her for two weeks?"

"Yes, she was held captive there, Thomas and Marcus were unable to track her, until you went missing. Thomas was able to track her to the woods. That is where Marcus picked up your trail." The tears spill from Sam's eyes as she talks about Mia. "She was no longer in her right mind when we got her out of their last night. Thomas had to put her out of her misery last night. No traces of her humanity were left. They had starved her and tortured her until she lost every sense, but survival. Mia didn't even recognize Thomas when he took her home." Sam sniffs and wipes the tears from her face. "We all aren't like that, Jas. We maintain our humanity. We know love and hurt, but what they did to her drove her crazy."

"Sam, I'm sorry about Mia." The tears rimming my eyes spill down my cheeks. This woman is my friend, regardless of what she is.

"It doesn't matter now." Sam shrugs her shoulders. "She is in a better place, anyway, I wanted you to know, she wouldn't have done that two weeks ago. Mia was a kind soul and she loved life. Jas, Allya and I we care about you. We would never hurt you, but you still have a choice. Marcus loves you. You can still chose to join us or go on with your life now. No one will hurt you, regardless of your choice."

"Sam, I don't know what to do. I'm still confused and scared. You guys killed those men last night." I curl my knees to my chest, rocking in my chair. My heart hurts, for my love, my friends, but fear rules my mind.

"I understand, but know that those men hunt us. They search us out, and kill any of us they come across. They tortured Mia for two weeks, to find new weaknesses in our species. They will kill the shifter children. They do not care who we are, the hunter groups kill all supernatural beings." Sam gets up, pulling Allya up beside her.

"Sam?" I stand facing her. "Why did Marcus pick me?"

"That's his story Jas, I can't tell you that." Sam takes Allya's hand and they walk out the door.

Allya was quiet during this conversation. She never said another word to me after her announcement of being a shifter. I watch as the two of them head out into the night, leaving me alone with my jumbled mind again.

My mind is exhausted. Heading up to bedroom, I throw the robe in the corner. I slip into the bed and allow sleep to drag me under.

The cool night air caresses my skin, raising goose bumps. The moon hangs high in the sky, the singing of the wolves ringing in my ears. The warm breathe of a lover skates across the back of my neck. I turn sliding my arms around the neck of my love, looking into the amber gaze. A whispering of love, of promise, sealed with a passionate kiss. ' I shall love you for eternity, following your soul across time and space. For one day, you will be ready to join me again.' My lover tells me as he pulls me hard against his body. He draws my tongue into his mouth, running hot hands across my back. He pulls away from me, tears glistening in his perfect eyes. Then he is gone. I am alone in the darkness and the wolves sing a sorrowful tune.

I land on the floor next to the bed with a thud. My body shaking, tears streaming down my face. My heart hurts. The empty ache strangles the air from my lungs. I gasp for breath, sobs wracking my body, heaving as the air rushing into my lungs. My throat constricts. I need to see him. The man in my dreams with the whiskey eyes, I need to know.

Chapter 23

There's a commotion at the front of the bar. Jake is arguing with someone who sounds determined to get in. I walk over that way and catch a glimpse of my beautiful brunette in all of her five foot six inch stature pointing in Jake's face and yelling to see me right now. Jake looks bewildered, and trying hard to cover a smirk. She Jasmine looks quite the sight: hand on her hip, finger shaking furiously. I do believe if Jake cracks that smile she may punch him in the mouth.

Deciding to intervene, saving him from the wrath of my little woman, I tell him, "It is fine, Jake, I'm already awake this evening." Turning to her, I drink in her beauty. "Hello Jasmine. You are early." The look she gives me could melt glaciers. She stalks across the waiting room to me, placing her hands back on her hips. She thrusts a finger against my chest.

"We need to talk. You have a lot of explaining to do." She stomps ahead of me into the bar.

"Jasmine, love, please sit down.

"Here drink this." I hand her the wine. She smiles up at me with her tear stained face. She sips the wine, taking a few deep breaths.

She just sits there sipping her wine, staring into it, finally her breathing is returning to normal and her heart ceases its rapid pounding. She looks up at me and I'm shocked at the depth of love I see on her face. She is radiant.

"Marcus, I love you, but we need to talk about a few things. I'm still afraid but I don't want to go on without you." The tears leak freely from her eyes. The uncertainty blatantly displayed on her face. "I don't ever want to not know what we found together this week. Just thinking about not being with you makes my heart, my soul ache."

I feel the same way when she leaves in the wee hours of the morning. I didn't want to rush her though so I stayed away from her and let her make her own choices.

"I love you too my sweet, I don't want to ever be without you."

"I need you to tell me what happened the other night?" She shifts in her seat, her voice quivering with fear.

My heart sinks, knowing I am the cause of the fear shooting through her body. Her fingers tremble, as she holds the stem of the wine glass. This is my fault.

"Jasmine, I'm sorry you had to see me like that. I didn't mean to be so out of control."

"It's just, Marcus I don't understand your world. I don't know why you picked me?" Her voice quivers.

"I was lost when you went missing. I could no longer control the animal within myself. When I found you and Mia was hurting you. I lost the little control I had left. I snapped."

"Marcus, why did you kill those men?"

"They took you away from me. I was angry, but not only that. They had Mia for two weeks. Did you see the shape she was in?" I reach for her hand, stroking my thumb along her knuckles. She doesn't pull away.

"Sam and Allya stopped by last night. Sam told me what they did to Mia. Marcus I'm sorry for the loss of your friend, but I don't understand this war between your kind and the hunters." Jasmine levels her gaze on me, a look of need and sorrow in her eyes.

"The hunters believe we are the devil incarnate, set upon the world as a plague. They hunt us to the ends of the earth killing all of us they find." I take her hand in mine, willing her to understand. " Yes, we do drink blood and we do kill for it however, most of us prey on the scum of society. Thieves, junkies, and drug dealers cleaning up the streets making them safer for the rest of you."

"I see." Her face masks her emotions. "Can you give me one more day to make this decision?"

"Yes, my love is eternal."

"What did you say?" Jasmine's heart accelerates, as she stares at me.

"My love is eternal."

Jasmine bites her lip and her eyes dart across my face. Her breathing comes in shallow gasps. She rings her hands together.

"Is there another question on your mind?" I gently probe for the question she needs to ask. I have an idea of what it could be, but I need her to get it out on her own time.

"Marcus how many times have we been down this road? I dreamed of you last night. I think the girl was me. I don't remember those lives, but I felt your sadness, your pain when I died."

"I am two hundred years old my love, we have been together four times. I've found you every time, but you were never ready to live with me eternally." She has never recalled our past together before. Destiny is finally intervening on my behalf thank the Gods.

"I want to be with you eternally." Her breathing quickens to almost a panicked state. "I want to make this change with you. There are things I can't leave behind. There is my shop. I need someone to take care of it during the day." She chews her lip. The worry, furrowing across her brow. "I can still run the internet orders on my own. I really would like someplace I can still grow the herbs and flowers I use to make my poultices."

"That won't be a problem, everyone here is not a vampire, some are shifters, they run the bar for me during the day doing orders or meetings for me." I take her hand in mine again. These are minor things she worries about. I can take care of all of that for her." I'm sure we will be able to find a few to run your shop for you during the day. I own a bit of property outside of town too. I could build you a greenhouse with artificial sunlight to grown your herbs in and the house on the property has a huge kitchen for you to make anything you wish. It can be your own little haven for herbs."

The look she gives me is pure bliss and lights up her whole face.

"Marcus I always wanted a greenhouse. I've never had the space for one before. That would be amazing."

" I will do whatever you want to make you happy my love." I stand and pull her into my arms.

"When do you want to turn me? Is it going to hurt?" Jasmine gazes up into my face, her eyes echoing the uncertainty of her voice.

"I was thinking about turning you tonight, unless you would like to wait some, but the sooner the better. I am barely in control around you now. Since you have agreed I don't know how long I can hold onto that control." Taking her hand in mine, I kiss the palm. "No, it won't hurt, you won't be any different from yourself now except stronger, faster, your eyes will glow, and fangs will grow. You will wake up hungry, but I won't let you do it alone. I'll teach you to hunt, to feed, and I'll be with you every step of the way."

She seems happy with those answers, but she has gone quiet.

"Have you bitten me before?"

"Yes, I have and you enjoyed it. I've never hurt you my love, you are my heart and soul."

"Can we go to your room now?" She lowers her gaze to the floor, her voice so soft if I were human I wouldn't have heard her.

"Yes." I take her hand leading her to the back elevator and take her to my room.

Chapter 24

The butterflies decide that now is the best time to dance the polka in my stomach as we ride the elevator up to his suite. I want this, I do, but I'm terrified of change. I hold onto him as a lifeline, crushing myself against his body. He is a warm, solid, and comforting presence next to me. He says nothing as we ride up to his room. When the bell dings are arrival, the doors slide open, he gently ushers me inside. Marcus leads me into the open plan living room sitting me on the leather sofa facing the huge bay window. I never noticed the window before. I wouldn't think vampires would have windows in their homes, at least not this big.

"It has ultra violet light filters in the glass. I can see a sunrise if I wish too. The daylight makes us tired and we need to rest. Sunlight can be dangerous to us, so I think calling us to sleep is nature's way of protecting us. I am old enough that I can fight the drag of sleep if need be." The melody of his voice washes over me, soothing my fraying nerves. The idea that I can still watch the sunrise is appealing to me. "When you turn you will be very tired at sunrise for a few years yet. You will however at least be able to stay awake long enough to watch the sky turn from twilight to pink and yellow before you need to sleep. You can sleep here with me or we can always move to the house on the property outside of town. All of the properties I own have the same glass installed so they are safe houses for all of our kind. The shifters maintain the lands for me. Their packs are safe here too. We work together to keep the human's from finding out about us." He paces in front of the window. I think he's as nervous about this as I am.

"Marcus, come sit with me." I pat the couch beside me.

I need to be close to him, to reaffirm my choice to be here. I want this. I know what I'm getting into nothing else matters as long as we do it together.

He sits down beside me on the couch and I crawl into his lap. He wraps his strong arms around me and just holds me there. His scent is intoxicating as I inhale the aroma of him from his neck where I bury my head. He is safe, my home. That's, all I need to know. I kiss his neck feeling his responding growl rumble deep in his chest. No more encouragement needed, I continue my exploration, kissing my way up his neck and across his jawline. I pepper kisses around his mouth before slanting mine across his. He opens to me and I slide my tongue inside tasting the red wine he has been drinking. His grip on me tightens. I feel his cock grow hard under my ass. Marcus runs his hand up my back, grabbing my shoulders to pull me away.

"Jasmine, are you sure about this?" His eyes searching my face. The need in his voice is my undoing.

"Yes, Marcus. I am, turn me now, tonight. We'll figure out the rest later. I need to be with you." I lean into him, sliding my tongue along his lips. I can't wait any longer I need him to seal our relationship for all of eternity.

Marcus picks me up carrying me to the bedroom, laying me on the bed. He strokes my body, as if I am made of china and will shatter beneath him. The things we have done seem not to matter in this moment. He pulls the hem of my tank up my body kissing every inch of skin it reveals, I lean up so he can pull it over my head. He leans down brushing his lips across mine pushing me back onto the bed. He kisses his way down my neck only stopping to lavish attention onto each nipple, turning them into hard peaks before he continues his downward travel across my stomach. He unzips my jeans and slowly peels them from my body. He removes my shoes. I'm completely naked under his molten gaze.

His eyes are glowing and his fangs are peeking out of his closed lips. He leans down running his hot tongue across my slit. I moan my approval and thrust my hips up seeking more contact. He backs away, not willing to be rushed. He doesn't restrain me and there is no blindfold. He moves up my body until he lay over me. Marcus braces his arms on either side of me head, the muscles in his arms flex, rippling with the effort. He kisses me softly, before slanting his lips over mine deepening the kiss until I can no longer think clearly, lost in the sensations; the taste of him.

He strips his clothes off without breaking the kiss, his hardened cock rubs my slit, seeking entrance. I open my legs allowing him total access. His entrance is slow and torturous, as he fills me inch by inch. Marcus takes his time in fulfilling the ache in my womb, once fully seated he ends our kiss, looking deep into my eyes, seeing the love and adoration, knowing I'm making the right choice. He pulls his cock almost all the way out and pushes back in. It is a slow love making, one for the history books. I feel the build of orgasm burning a slow fire in my belly, coiling tight, ready to burst forth.

Marcus keeps me on the edge of the cliff ready to fall, to fly into oblivion with him. He leans back and pulls me into his arms. My legs over his sitting in his lap, he guides my hips onto his cock, reaching deeper into my soul with every thrust. I'm going to come. His eyes flash, and his shaft swells inside of me, his orgasm is upon him too.

I bare my neck to him, throwing my head back. The prick of his fangs into me, the sudden euphoria from the first pull of my blood into his mouth sends me careening into a mind-blowing orgasm. I shudder and pulse around his cock, each pull of his mouth on my neck sending mini shock waves coursing through my body. His own orgasm overtakes him as his cock pulses and throbs into my pussy filling me with his seed.

I awake to him feeding me blood from his wrist. I don't feel any different, but then again, waking to feeding on blood isn't exactly normal. I'm so hungry. I continue to feast from his wrist. The pungent coppery flavor tastes of mulled wine spiked with cloves. The overwhelming scent of sandalwood and leather fill my brain. . My pussy clenches with the need for him, not just his blood.

Marcus pulls his wrist away from my lips and wipes

my chin of the blood running down it. He smiles at me, a truly happy content smile. I'm his. I turned and we will be together forever. The impact of what we have done finally hits home as he sits there staring at me and I start to cry. Tears stream down my face as I look at him. The man, who made me, wants me for all time. Who will love me like no other. I'm happier in this moment than I have ever been in my whole life.

I launch myself into his arms, kissing and holding him, I wrap myself around his body. The laugh that rumbles out of his chest is pure ecstasy. He holds me tight kissing me back. We are two souls no longer lost, but found in the arms of each other.

Chapter 25

Jasmine has been a vampire for two weeks and tonight, Sam and I are taking her to the streets to go hunting. We have been supplying her blood at the bar until this point, working on her learning her new abilities.

"Sam are you sure she's ready?" I pace around the living room of the farmhouse, waiting for Jasmine to come downstairs.

"Marcus she has been ready. You need to let her learn to hunt properly."

" I know Sam. Damn it, I want to protect her."

"Well teaching her to hunt is protecting her." Sam turns to me putting her hands on her hips.

The rustle at the top of the stairs draws my attention from Sam. Jasmine stands at the top, her dark hair cascading around her shoulders, her brown eyes glowing with hunger. She leaps from the top landing directly in front of me, wrapping her body around me. Her mouth covers mine, as she devours my lips, thrusting her tongue into my mouth. She growls deep in her throat, eliciting a resounding growl from me.

"I want to go hunting Marcus." She slithers her body against me, purring her request.

"Yes my love, we will take you."

Sam's laugh jolts me back to reality, realizing I've been conned by my mate.

"Jasmine you are being very naughty." I raise my eyebrow, leveling my gaze on her. " I believe you need a reminder, when we return."

"Yes Sir." Jasmine lowers her gaze to the floor.

I grasp her chin tilting her head to look at me again. The smirk on her face heightens my arousal. She enjoys submission and loves to ruffle my feathers. " You my love are a handful." I grab her hand leading her out the door and into the night.

The three of us touch down in my favorite alley. There are always low lifes hanging out in this area. Jasmine's still a bit squeamish about killing.

"Are you ready?" I turn to her.

"I got this." She nods her head.

Sam and I follow Jasmine into the alley, letting her scent and listen for the prey. She will pick the one tonight on her own. I watch as her head cocks to the side, she hears the heart beat in the back. Jasmine licks her lips, as her fangs grow. Her eyes flit from side to side, searching the darkness. A growl rumbles from her chest as she darts into the back of the alley. Sam and I take off after her. We come to the corner of the buildings. Jas has a man by the throat, holding him in the air, as she taunts him.

"What's the matter? You don't want to smack me around too?" Jasmine shakes the man from side to side.

He grunts an inaudible answer, as Jasmine squeezes tighter on his windpipe. His face turns a ruddy red. I know the moment she bares her fangs. The pimp's eyes, grow wide and he pisses himself. Jasmine lunges at him, sinking her fangs into his neck. His legs flail uselessly in the trash around him. Jasmine drops his lifeless body onto the ground, turning to me. Blood dribbles down her chin, she bares her teeth in a smile. Her tongue darts out licking the blood drops from her lips. I take her in my arms, running my tongue along the path of blood from her chin to her lips.

"I want more Marcus."

"Jasmine love, we still need to find two more, you didn't save any for Sam and I."

"I'm sorry, I am so hungry." She hangs her head.

"Love, you will never go without. Now come on find Sam and I something to eat."

Jasmine bounds off into the night, stalking the alleys for more prey.

Sam smacks me on the back and chuckles. " You got your hands full."

"You aren't telling me anything new." I head out of the alley.

Jasmine catches three more drug dealers out tonight. She loves the hunt. I have never seen a fledgling vampire hone their skills so quickly. Sam and I dispose of the bodies tonight, since Jas did the tracking. Sam heads over to the club, she has moved into the condo above, now that Jas and I live in the farmhouse.

Jasmine takes my hand as we enter the house. Her smile, devilish. "What can I do to make you forgive me for earlier? Master."

"Are you sure you want to play that game tonight." I pull her hair, yanking her head back, licking the pulse in her neck.

"Mmmmm, yes." She arches against me, moaning.

I push her to her knees. She slides her hands up my legs, traveling towards the buttons on my pants. Jasmine makes quick work of opening the buttons and slips her hands inside. She wraps her fingers around my shaft. She smiles up at me, mischief sparkling in her eyes. She frees my shaft, licking her lips as it comes into view. She swirls her tongue around the head, working her hand up and down it's length.

"Open your mouth love." I twine my fingers in her hair.

She obediently opens her mouth and I thrust to the back of her throat. Her eyes fill with tears as she gags, but she doesn't pull away. I fuck her mouth, in quick hard strokes, using her hair to move her head. She digs her nails into my thighs, raking welts across them. The scent of her arousal surrounds me. My shaft swells in her warm wet mouth. She sucks hard on my cock as I thrust in quick short strokes. I jerk hard on her hair, pulling her towards me, as I bury my cock deep in her throat. My cock pulses as I empty my release in her mouth. She looks up at me and smiles, licking the salty drops from her lips.

"Does that please you? Master." She stands, purring in my ear.

"It does my love, but you are going without tonight." I stroke her hair, stifling a smile at her pouting face. "Come love, the sun will be up soon." I lead her up the stairs to our bedroom.

"Do I have to go without?" She thrusts her bottom lip out.

"What do you think?"

"I know, but you can't blame me for trying." She lies down in the bed curling into my arms.

Chapter 26

It's been two months since my changing. I love Marcus more every night. Our days are spent sleeping in each other's arms. The nights full of hunting and sex. Sam and Allya will be here soon. It's going to be girl's night. The first one since our spa day. Marcus has a meeting with Anthony tonight. So the girls are going to hang out.

"Hey, I'm so glad you gals made it tonight." I wrap my arms around both women.

"So where are we setting up this party." Sam jiggles a cooler.

"Let's go upstairs, Marcus has a meeting tonight with Anthony."

"Anthony is here?" Allya's eyes dart around the room.

"Yeah why?" I grab Allya's shoulders, forcing her to look at me.

"Uh, no reason."

"Okay then, let's go upstairs. I have some news." I grab both their hands and pull them up the steps.

I drag the women into the bedroom and slam the door. The excitement threatens to burst from my chest. My heart races pounding out a staccato beat in my chest, and my head spins.

"Damn woman what has got you all worked up?" Sam dumps the cooler on the floor and sits next to me.

"We have a wedding to plan." I hold up my hand showing her the gold and diamond ring. "Marcus gave it to me last night."

"That's great." Allya grabs me in a crushing hug.

"Wow, that's beautiful." Sam holds my hands studying the ring.

"So when are you planning the ceremony?" Allya sits on the other side of me.

"Well I don't have a date yet, but I'm thinking next month. I want you both to be in it."

"That sounds like fun." Sam hugs me tight against her. I can see the longing her on face.

"What all did you bring in the cooler?"

"AB and O positive." Sam flips the lid pulling out the bags.

I can't stop the laughter that bubbles out. I fall back on the bed holding my stomach as I lose my control. Sam just smiles. Allya throws a pillow at her and things are normal once again. Regaining some form of composure. I sit up.

"Sam can I ask you something?"

"Yeah Jas, what's up?" She opens one of the bags, sucking the contents out.

"The night you saved me, did you get all the hunters?" I watch her face intently for clues, but she masks all her emotions.

"No we didn't, one of the redneck boys got away. Why do you ask? Has something happened?" Sam's eyes bore into me, like she's trying to read my soul.

"Nothing happened, I was just wondering, you know,

if we are safe or if they could still come after us." I lie back on the bed and stare at the ceiling.

"Marcus isn't going to let anything happen to you, Jas." Sam lies down beside me.

"We won't let anything happen to you either." Allya lies on the other side of me.

"Enough of this talk, what color are you planning for the wedding?" Sam rolls over propping her head up on her hand.

"I was thinking black and gold. What kind of dresses do you guys want to wear? You can each pick your own style."

" I want to wear a sweet heart neckline with a full skirt, strapless." Allya stands up, twirling around the room.

" I want long sleeves, and a full skirt." Sam opens another bag of blood. "What are you going to wear?"

"I haven't decided yet."

"Who is Marcus having in the wedding?" Allya stops her twirling to look at me.

"I am pretty sure Anthony and Michael will be standing with him." I look at both girls sensing the shock flood their systems. "Alright spill it. You first Allya."

"Nothing really, it's not that I dislike Anthony personally or anything. Alpha wolves make me nervous." She fidgets with her hands refusing to make eye contact.

"Allya you're a wolf, why do wolves make you nervous"

"I don't want to talk about it right now, please."

Allya's eyes fill with tears.

"Okay don't cry, we don't have to talk about it tonight, but can you manage to get through the ceremony beside him?"

"I can do that, for you Jas." She smiles.

"Sam what about you, why do you not like Michael?"

"It's nothing against him, I just well damn it. He's my soul mate Jas." She covers her face with the pillow.

"Sam! Why didn't you tell me? Isn't that a good thing?" I pull the pillow from her.

"No it's not a good thing. He stares at me in the club and his blood calls to me. I didn't think I would ever find my soul mate. I don't know if I'm ready for a mate."

"Sam if anyone deserves their soul mate it's you." I pull her into an embrace.

"He's a Dom, Jas." Her voice waivers. "He's also a shifter, what if I'm not his mate?"

I understand her reluctance now, knowing some of her history. I don't know Michael that well, but all the men I've met in Marcus's circle would never hurt a woman.

"Sam, I don't think that will be a problem." I push her back looking into her eyes. "Take the time at the wedding to get to know him. There will be a lot of people around so you can talk in the open, no pressure."

"Okay, I will try, but enough talk about us, Let's plan your wedding." Sam gives me a little smile and grabs the note pad. "Time to make a list of what you're going to need."

We spend the rest of the night laughing and making

lists. We have guests list, seating arrangements, and flowers. We are going to go dress shopping next weekend. The girls are wearing black dresses and I am wearing a gold one. Sam knows a hairdresser that will do home appointments so she is going to book her tomorrow. Since she can stay awake longer than I can at sunrise. Allya has volunteered to do all the shopping in town for decorations and lights, since she can go out in the daytime. Things are coming along nicely. My best friends and I are planning the perfect day with my eternal love.

Chapter 27

Today is my wedding day. Allya arrives shortly after Sam. We are in the upstairs bedroom getting dressed for the day.

"The backyard looks amazing Jas." Allya zips up the back of her dress.

"Are you sure?" My voice waivers.

"Jas, it's going to be perfect." Sam zips the back of my dress up, pulling my hair out of the way.

"I couldn't do this without you guys." I wipe the tears from my eyes.

"No crying, not yet, you'll ruin your make-up." Allya grabs a tissue blotting my eye.

I take a deep breath, fanning my face, attempting to stop the flow of tears. My best friends are here to get me through today. I'm marring the man of my dreams, literally. The music floats into the window from the yard. The enchanting melody, soothing my fraying nerves.

"It's time to go." Allya hands me my flowers and kisses my cheek.

"Okay, see you girls at the altar." I nod my head, taking the flowers from her.

The rhythmic bridal march starts, after Allya and Sam exit the back door. My turn. I walk in time to the beat, eying my perfect mate amongst the twinkling lights. The lighting that adorns the back yard makes me feel like walking though the night sky Marcus waits at the end of the isle his eyes glowing a fiery amber. His smile warms my heart, and quickens my breath.

I reach the end of the walkway, taking my place beside him in the front. Marcus takes my hand in his, peering at me from lowered lashes. His eyes blaze a trail of need through my body, igniting a burn of desire in my belly.

The high priest drones on about the sanctity of our vows. The eternal love of soul mates and the promise to keep each other first always. I only hear about half of what he is saying, as I lose myself in the warmth of my love.

He holds a slim gold band in his hand; my fingers tremble as he recites his vow to me.

"Jasmine, this ring is eternal, no beginning and no ending. I promise to love you as eternal as this circle. For now until the end of all time." Marcus slips the golden band on my trembling finger.

"Marcus, my love for you has been eternal, even if I couldn't remember before. You are the man of my dreams. The man who I will love eternally for now and until the end of time." I slip the band onto his hand.

"You may now kiss your bride." The high priest turns to Marcus.

Marcus pulls me flush against his body, slanting his mouth over mine. The gentle press of his lips against me dissolves my awareness of anything, but him. His tongue probes my lips seeking entrance. I open to him, tasting the unique flavors of my love. My body sways into him, as his strong arms wrap around me, surrounding me with his scent.

Marcus breaks the kiss, pulling back away from me. The sounds of catcalls and hollers bring me back to the present. Heat flames my face, as I stare at my toes, hiding from the audience. He pulls me to stand beside him, rubbing his thumb across my knuckles. The comforting touch, soothing my embarrassment. Marcus leads me back down the walkway as the audience blows a sea of bubbles into our walkway.

Anthony cleared the chairs out of the way, making room for the DJ to set up and the food to be placed out for the reception. The crowd gathers around Marcus and I waiting for the toss of the bouquet and apparently my garter I turn my back on the crowd of girls, peeking over my shoulder to wink at Sam and Allya. I throw the bundle of black lilies over my shoulder. The sound of wresting and giggling reach my ears. I turn smiling to look at a shocked faced Sam, holding the bundle of flowers. I run off the steps launching myself into her arms, hugging her tight. I pull back and look at her, she smiles, but tears threaten to fall from her eyes.

"Jas, I'm scared." Her voice quivers.

"It will be all right hon."

Marcus pulls me back up the stairs to his side. He slips his hand under the hem of my dress, trailing his fingers over my skin. Goosebumps break out on my body, my legs tremble under his touch. He slides the garter down my leg, as woohoos come from the crowd.

He turns his back to the men, flinging the ring of satin and lace over his shoulder. Michael catches it and winks at Marcus.

The DJ strikes up a slow song. The soft melody flows through my body. Marcus takes my hand leading me into the center of the yard. He pulls me into his arms and we sway to the music. He looks into my eyes and the love I see there takes my breath away. I lay my head on his shoulder, trusting him to lead me safely in the dance. Our bodies meld into each other, a perfect fit of hard planes and soft curves.

The music changes to something faster and we are surrounded by a sea of bodies. Marcus pulls me to the edge of the swarm of people all rubbing together in the center of the yard.

"Come on love, let's get you something to eat."

"That sounds like a wonderful idea."

He takes my hand leading me to the buffet tables set up across from the DJ booth. There is an array of finger foods to choose from. Steak tar-tar, smoked salmon crepes with dill sauce, and stuffed mushrooms. There are glasses of champagne stacked in a pyramid with the server pouring the bubbling gold liquid into the top glass, creating a fountain of alcohol into the rest of them. It's the most romantic scene I've ever seen. I lean up on my toes, kissing Marcus on the cheek.

"Thank you, for making this night so special." The tears fall freely from my eyes.

"Awe, my love, I would do anything for you." He wipes the tears from my cheeks and pulls me into his arms. "Now my dear, eat something."

I fill a plate with a little of everything and carry a glass of champagne over to the garden bench. I nibble each item, savoring the delicate balance of flavors. The smoky salmon with the creamy dill sauce, by far my favorite item here tonight. The bubbles from the champagne tickle my nose.

The crowd has paired off into intimate groups, chatting amongst themselves. People are smiling and laughing, having a generally good time. I spy Allya in the corner a frown on her pretty face. I follow her line of sight. She is boring holes in Anthony's back. He turns and waves at her, offering a welcoming smile. She crosses her arms over her chest and stalks in the opposite direction of him.

"Geez, she didn't look to happy about that."

"Who are you talking about?" Marcus turns to face me.

"Oh, I was people watching. Allya was glaring at Anthony, but when he turned to wave at her, well she looked pissed and stormed off." I shrug my shoulders, not really understanding why she hates Alpha males so much.

"To each their own, I guess. Maybe she will come around." He wraps his arm around my shoulders pulling me against him.

"Did you see who caught the flowers and garter?"

"Yes I did."

"Did you throw the garter to Michael on purpose." I sit up to look into his face.

"Now Jasmine I can't believe you would think I would do that." He holds his hands to his heart, feigning hurt.

"I take that as a yes." I smack his arm as laughter bursts from his lips.

"I had to help them out." He pulls me into his arms, brushing his lips over mine. "Everyone should be this happy."

" I agree with that."

"I need to go and talk to Anthony will you miss me?" He smiles.

"Always my love."

I watch him walk away, his suit cut to a perfect fit on his body. It highlights the broad shoulders, trim waist, and amazing ass. I think the champagne is getting to me. I don't care this is my night. I walk over to the table, selecting another glass.

Sam is in the corner of the walkway by the gate to leave. I head over that way, but halt my approach when I see Michael around the corner. Sam is shaking her head no, but Michael just smiles, rubbing his hands on her shoulders. Her body tenses, like she is about to run. He pulls her towards him and captures her lips in his. I turn to give them privacy and head back to my garden bench.

Thomas is sitting on the bench across from me. His eyes, red and sore. He lost his best friend this week. He gets up and stumbles towards the table, taking an entire bottle of champagne from the server. He pops the cork and chugs directly from the bottle. He staggers back to his bench, with sadness etched into his face. My heart breaks for him. I wish I knew him better, to offer some comfort, but it was my ex that caused it. Guilt encompasses me freezing me to my spot. I have no words to soothe his pain.

Jake strolls off of the dance floor sitting next to Thomas on the bench, taking the bottle from his hand. Thomas grabs for it, falling onto the ground. Jake picks him up and carries him out the gate. I hope he will be able to take care of him tonight.

Marcus sits on the bench next to me. "Why the sad face, love?"

"Thomas looked so sad tonight. I feel guilty for his loss." I wrap my arms around myself in an attempt to quell the shivers in my soul.

"Jasmine, what happened with Mia wasn't your fault." Marcus pulls me onto his lap, resting my head on his shoulder. "Thomas doesn't blame you. Hell Mia almost killed you too."

"Yeah, I guess." Shivers wrack my body, as memories of Mia sinking her teeth into my neck return.

"Come dance with me love. Enjoy our night. I love you. Eternally." He stands, lifting me up and carrying me to the dance area.

"I love you too and I am eternally yours."

We dance and laugh the rest of the night. Marcus doesn't give me a chance to stop and think about anyone, but him the rest of the night. He leads me inside as the sky starts to lighten. The impending sunrise, ending the party. The shifters agree to clean up. Marcus settles me in our bed tucking me into the soft warm covers.

"Sleep well my love." He kisses me softly.

The call of sleep drags me under and for once I don't dream about the amber-eyed man. I've no need to dream of him anymore, I shall have him in my waking hours, side by side. Two hearts, two kindred spirits. I was lost until he found me, the fates allowing us to return to one another, for eternity.

Epilogue

It's midnight at the club, Sam hasn't talked to me since I kissed her at the wedding a month ago. I should never have kissed her, but she is the most beautiful creature I had ever laid eyes on. Her strength and her love of friends and family called to my inner wolf. She spends all her time brooding and sulking around the club. Her scenes with the fledgling vamps are getting more and more out of control. That is when she does play. Most of the time she just sits at the bar, downing shots and ignoring everyone around her. She isn't playing tonight, just throwing back shot, one after another.

I walk over to the bar, placing my hand on her shoulder. Her body tenses, the scent of adrenaline pouring off her in waves. "Sam, what seems to be bothering you? You haven't been yourself lately."

She turns to me, her emerald eyes sparkling with unshed tears. "Can we go and talk somewhere else? Will you come up to the suite and talk to me. I really need a friend right now."

How can I say no to her? She is the most beautiful woman I've ever seen, everything about her screams perfection. She wants me to be alone with her. My cock throbs against my zipper. I need to get my raging libido under control. The last thing Sam needs right now is a horny werewolf panting down her neck. She turned me down at the wedding.

"Yes, let me find Anthony and let him know I'm going to break. I'll meet you at the elevator." I stand up and head throw the grinding bodies of leather, searching for him.

We ride up the elevator in complete silence, the only noise is the clicking of her nails against one another. She fidgets, shifting her weight back and forth on her feet. The dinging bell announces our arrival. I follow her into the suite. She has replaced all of Marcus's furniture. The couches are sleek black leather, with red and turquoise accent pillows. The coffee table is a solid piece of carved black stone. The whole room screams Sam. She leads me over to the sofa sitting down and patting the spot next to her.

"Sam, what is going on? " I put my hand on her leg, to comfort her.

"Michael, I'm so unhappy, it takes everything I have not to walk into the sunrise and never come back. "The tears stream down her cheeks.

"What makes you so sad, that you would end it all?" I turn her to face me.

"I'm jealous of the love Marcus and Jasmine have. I'm happy for them, but I want that too. What's wrong with me Michael? Why can't I find what I need to be complete?" Her body shakes with sobs.

"Sam, there is nothing wrong with you. You are perfect." I pull her into my arms, hugging her tight.

The scent of her overwhelms me. That undeniable shifter sensation floods my being. My wolf screaming in my head. MINE, MATE, CLAIM. This is already a bad situation and now this. Why didn't I get this feeling at the wedding? I would have at least been prepared. I'm second in command of the pack and unmated, but Sam is in no shape for me to be staking claims.

She brushes feather light kisses along my jawline, working her way to my mouth. She licks my lips seeking entrance. I open allowing her inside. Her taste floods my being, mint and chocolate. My cock aches for release. Her arms wrap around my neck as she twine her fingers in my hair, pulling me hard against her mouth.

I push her away. "Sam I have to go."

The shock and hurt that crosses her face, break my heart. It burns an image in my brain that will haunt me forever. I run to the elevator, banging on the button. The wolf in me growls, urging me to go back and claim my mate. The doors slide open and I climb inside. The last thing I see as the doors close, is Sam rubbing her lips, her sad eyes watching me run away.

How will I ever explain why I left? She needs a friend and my damn wolf decides now is the time to make it's wants known. I want to go back up there and throw her to the ground, ravaging her body and claiming every inch of her as mine. I need to take this slow, she is hurting and I made it worse. This is fucked up beyond repair. Shit, I'm a Dom, vamps aren't submissive, are they? Sam's one hundred and fifty years old. I don't even know if she will ever speak to me again. She has trust issues and I just abandoned her when she needed me. I need to find Marcus. We have to talk.

I run out of the elevator, mentally shouting to Anthony that I am leaving. Marcus and Jasmine aren't at the club tonight. I bust out the doors of the club, the cool night air breaking through the pain in my soul from leaving my mate behind. I tear off my clothes and shift, running the entire way to the old farmhouse.

The wind whips through my fur, igniting my need to hunt. The scents of the night relax my body allowing my mind to calm. Now that I have left my mate behind, how in the hell do I convince her I would never hurt her? After seeing the pain etched on her magnificent features, how will I ever prove I can erase the demons she hides inside?